my life

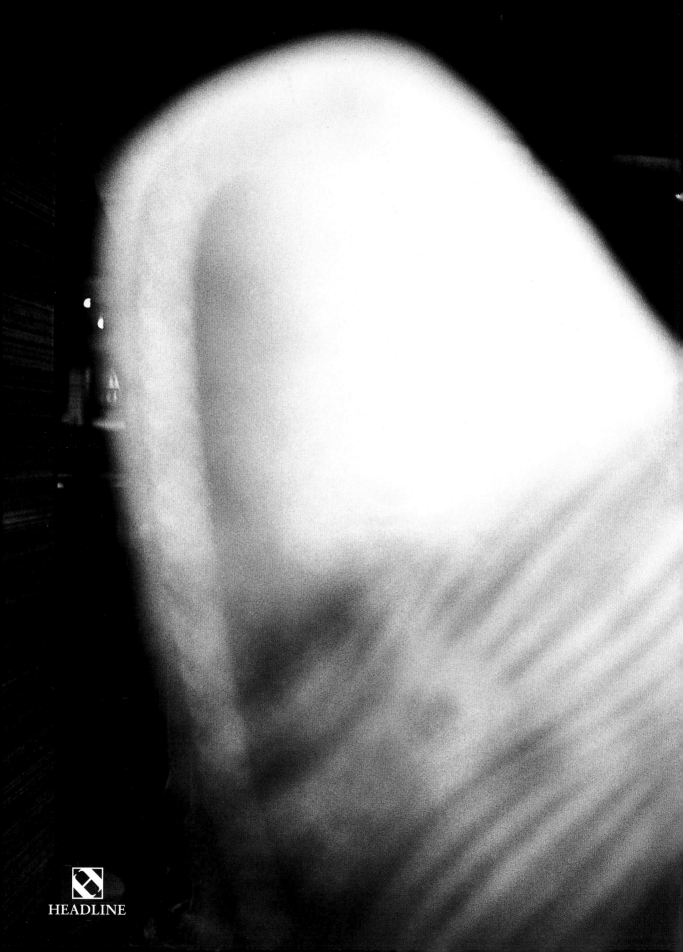

HEADLINE

Vinnie

my life: vinnie jones

First published in 2001
by HEADLINE BOOK PUBLISHING

10 9 8 7 6 5 4 3 2 1

British Library Cataloguing in Publication Data
Jones, Vinnie, 1965–
Vinnie: my life
1. Jones, Vinnie, 1965–
2. Soccer players – England – London – Biography
3. Soccer players – Wales – Biography
I. Title
796.3'34'092

ISBN 0 7472 4342 5

Designed by Mark Thomson,
International Design UK Ltd, London
Printed and bound in Great Britain
by Butler & Tanner Ltd, Frome, Somerset

HEADLINE BOOK PUBLISHING
A division of Hodder Headline
338 Euston Road
London NW1 3BH

www.headline.co.uk
www.hodderheadline.com

Picture credits
Actionimages: 100, 123t, 137, 163, 166
Allsport: 106, 148, 153, 165t | Camera Press: 185, 202, 219
Colorsport: 84, 109, 120, 123b, 165b | Frank Spooner
Pictures: 171, 221 | Katz Pictures: 223
Kobal Collection: 205b | Mission Pictures: 14, 193b, 194t,
195, 199, 200–1, 208, 209b, 217 | News Group
Newspapers/Linus Morran: 218 | PA: 10
Retna/Aujard/MPA: 1, 224 | Rex Features: 149
Ronald Grant Archive: 175, 176, 190, 193t |
Daniel Smith: 2–3 | Sygma: 6
Syndication International: 97 | UPPA: 8–9, 205t

To Granddad Arthur:
I just hope I am everything he hoped I would be as his eldest grandson.
And in memory of my good friend Brian Hall.

Acknowledgements

My thanks to Derek French, Dave Bassett, Don Howe,
John and Wendy Moore, Howard Wilkinson, Mike Hennigan,
Leeds United supporters, Joe Kinnear, John Fashanu,
Sam Hammam, all other supporters I have played for
and the players I have played with.

And thanks, of course, to Mum, Dad, Nan Ann, and the rest of
my family, including the Lamonts, Peter Burrell, all my friends
from Bedmond. And to John and Jo Sadler for their help
in writing my autobiography.

And special thanks to Tanya, Kaley and Aaron who are
the three most important people in my life.

Contents

Previous pages: Filming a scene from *Snatch* with Dennis Farina in Hatton Garden, London.

Ecstatic after receiving my award for Best Actor at the Empire Film Awards, 2001.

The date will be imprinted on my mind for all time: 19 February 2001. And the venue: the Dorchester Hotel in London's Park Lane. It was the night when, almost in disbelief but bursting with pride and excitement, I heard actress Minnie Driver's magical announcement:

'And the winner is . . . Vinnie Jones.'

I had arrived at The Dorchester with my wife Tanya and friends for the annual Empire Film Awards, sponsored by the international magazine, but I never thought for a moment that I would top the voting as Best British Actor. How could I, when the list of nominations included names like Sir Michael Caine, Bob Hoskins, Jude Law and Robert Carlisle? I knew I'd done well in the part of Bullet-Tooth Tony in Snatch. The reviews had told me that, and the box-office success of the film had confirmed it, but to see my name alongside those of such distinguished and experienced star performers was more than I ever expected.

So I just went along to the awards ceremony more than happy to have been nominated at all. Tanz and I even had a couple of mini tiffs over it during the course of the evening. She kept telling me:

'I think you're going to win it, I really do.'

'Don't think like that,' I urged her. I didn't want Tanya or anybody else in our company to feel the slightest twinge of disappointment when all I felt was proud and honoured.

But when Minnie Driver made that short announcement … well, if I'd been slightly taller or the ceiling had been a little lower, the Dorchester would have been phoning the maintenance men to repair a hole in the roof. I was up like a moon probe blasting off the launch-pad, clenched fist pumping the air. You don't get time to think, so instinct takes over. I grabbed Tanya for a brief cuddle and then it was a case of rushing on to the stage, my mind in a whirl, and trying to think of something to say as I was handed a handsome glass trophy.

In the midst of the euphoria I remembered to make it clear that, despite what everyone had read in the newspapers, we would not be moving to Hollywood. We would be staying put at our home in Boxmoor, Herts. I thanked Tanz and the kids, because they were the ones who had done the hard work, having to travel back and forth to LA during my time filming in America before I made *Snatch*. I also had a word for Jamie Bell, who had won the Best Newcomer award for his performance in *Billy Elliot*. I told him I was sure it wouldn't be long before he was clutching the trophy they'd just given me.

Best British Actor. Just think. Not an Oscar, maybe, but an award that carries great prestige. And it was mine. What's more, that it had come so soon after all those years of ridicule and vilification as I tried to make a name for myself in professional football was incredible. Winning the FA Cup with little Wimbledon in 1988 was more than satisfying for me after all the stick I'd received, but this night at the Dorchester was something else entirely.

Like football, film-making is a team effort. If I had to draw some kind of parallel between film and football honours, then I suppose I'd say that winning the Best Actor award was the equivalent of being voted Man of the Match in a cup-winning team and receiving the Players' Player of the Year trophy all at the same time. As a footballer, if you were asked before the event if winning the FA Cup would do you for the rest of your career, you'd say yes. But once you've experienced success you want more and more. I won't be happy now until I have to build a new extension on my house to

accommodate more film trophies.

The Empire award reflected well on my family, too. They'd had to put up with so much during my time in football, and without their understanding, comfort and support, I wouldn't have been where I am now: happy and contented in my new career. I enjoy it so much that I can't wait for the next part, the next film, the next challenge.

As a footballer I was never the best, but many people did give me credit for always committing myself 100 per cent. I always wondered how Alan Shearer and others felt when they were voted the top performers in their profession. My accolade has come from a different industry, a different world, but I now know what it's really like to be told: 'You're the best.'

It is a great relief to be out from under the umbrella of football's authorities. I've had the space to spread my wings and I'm my own man now, far more in control of what is happening to me. I always felt they were just waiting for any opportunity to get me, although, looking back, I realise that a lot of it was my own doing. Going into movies and making a success of it in such a short time has lifted an enormous weight from my shoulders.

I have much more spare time, too. Time to accept an invitation to a week's golfing in Barbados, or to watch my greyhounds run. Or my racehorse, Sixty Seconds. I have no one to answer to except myself. If I want I can go down to the gym every day, play tennis every day, have a round of golf when I choose.

The only thing that peeves me is the way I am still referred to as 'the ex-footballer turned actor'. It's as if the press cannot mention your name without harking back to the past all the time: as if even while they are giving you credit for something they want to have a dig at you. I think what they would really like to say is 'the ex crap footballer turned actor'. But it's not something I lose a lot of sleep over.

I have a great lifestyle these days. We have our house in Boxmoor, which cost fortunes to extend and improve, and we're planning to build another on the coast in south-west Ireland. Four double bedrooms, all en-suite, in thirty acres, including a lake already stocked with trout. We'll have our own landing stage off the beach and there is more than enough room for the kids to roar around on their motorbikes and quad bikes. It will be a holiday place, really, and with Tanya's family being Irish we're hoping to have the place finished and get everybody there together for a good family Christmas.

Football can open a lot of doors, but my brief time in the movies has already brought me into contact with even more celebrities and distinguished people I am privileged to count among my friends.

Me and Jools Holland during rehearsals for my singing debut at a dinner in aid of the NSPCC in 2000.

I get involved in a lot of charity events, but one I particularly enjoyed was a dinner in aid of the NSPCC. I wasn't sure that I was going to, because before the event I had a phone call from the highly respected musician Jools Holland. He told me that quite a few people would be doing a turn at the dinner, and asked if I would sing 'Leroy Brown'. Although I was not too keen at first, after an hour rehearsing with Jools I cracked it. I had some hard acts to follow. From Formula 1 there was Damon Hill on guitar and Eddie Jordan on drums. Eric Clapton did two or three numbers. And I boomed out 'Bad, Bad Leroy Brown' accompanied by Jools on the piano and his nineteen-piece band. The jockey Frankie Dettori was supposed to join me early in the piece, but he didn't jump up until halfway through. He said afterwards that he wasn't going to risk it until I'd got the place rocking.

There's one photograph taken at that dinner that has appeared all over the place. It shows me chatting with Prince Andrew, who is grinning from ear to ear. The Prince was seated at our table – or perhaps I should say that we were seated at his. I knew him quite well by then, and I was well aware of his liking for a good joke. And that's the reason why he is grinning in that picture. I've never revealed the joke I was telling him, but this is what it was:

A burly debt-collector calls at a house hoping to pick up the ten grand owing. It's a massive, palatial house, and the door is answered by a little lad of no more than eight years old, wearing a cravat, velvet jacket, silk trousers and flash slippers. He has a Cuban cigar in one hand and a glass of brandy in the other.

'Is your dad in?' asks the debt-collector.

The kid looks at the cigar, then at the brandy, and then looks up and says: 'Does it look like he's fucking in?'

Andrew loved it.

I am prouder of myself these days than I've ever been before. It's not all plain sailing, of course. When I went out to film in the United States for the first time, I felt deeply isolated and lonely. It was a feeling I'd experienced before, in my early days with Leeds United. But once I got into it I made my mark, just as I did up there in West Yorkshire. To my mind, the next challenge is always the biggest, and 2001 looked set to be the defining year of my new career in films when I was given the starring role in a remake of the Burt Reynolds movie *Mean Machine*.

This Paramount production, with a budget of between $4 and $5 million dollars, is to be produced by Matthew Vaughn and directed by Barry Skolnik, as luck would have it a fanatical Leeds United supporter. Matthew and the director Guy Ritchie, who gave me my first break in *Lock, Stock and Two Smoking Barrels*, had always said to me: 'When you are ready, you do your own movie. Stars are made once they can carry a film.' Well, as Dean Meehan, I am involved in almost every scene. This is my fifth film, and in the first four I didn't have that many lines. This time I have a hell of a lot of dialogue to learn, but I've never been more excited about any job in my life.

The film is about a fallen football star who is believed to have thrown an England game against Germany. He ends up a broken man, serving a three-year prison stretch for drink-driving. In jail he is roughed up until he agrees to play for their football team. In one scene there is a practice match between the cons and the screws, and all I can say is that the fouls in that game make some of my past indiscretions on the pitch look angelic.

The sport in the Reynolds film was American football but I believe our version is going to have great appeal on both sides of the Atlantic, because it is not a film about soccer, it is a human-interest story. So I know that learning all those lines will only be part of the task. I have to master the mood and the manner of delivery as well. In America the great Robert Duvall said to me: 'Listen, Vinnie, I talk, you listen. I listen, you talk. That's acting.' I wasn't sure exactly what he meant at the time, but I am now. You're not thinking about the words – they just come out, providing you get the mood and the timing right. As I see it, acting is about behaving naturally in unnatural surroundings.

I think, I certainly hope, that *Mean Machine* will become something of a cult movie. It will be different: we've taken out a lot of the swearing and horrible stuff, so this one will be for the kids. I think youngsters will go crackers about it.

Listen to me going on about myself and my smashing family, just about secure for life now. I have an FA Cup-winner's medal and a Best Actor award in pride of place in my dining-room and I'm confidently predicting that my latest film will achieve cult status around the world. What a life. What a transformation. If you're wondering how it all began, then when you know, I don't suppose you'll believe it.

My 1964 Cadillac.

Chapter 1

Devil or Angel

I was seven years old. Just another kid in the street, an ordinary kid – apart from the fact that I was already pretty experienced with a shotgun. Shooting was in the family – my dad, Peter, spent just about every spare minute he had out in the countryside with his mates and their guns. Just another kid with hopes and dreams, often lost in his own little world of make believe, longing one day to be as good as the Brazilian footballers we pretended we were. Our goalposts might only have been a couple of jumpers chucked on the ground at the local 'rec', but to us, it was the World Cup finals and just as serious as the real thing.

But one day I shattered my own childhood peace of mind. This mistake, at the age of seven, taught me a painful lesson that still hurts whenever I remember it – the first good hiding from my dad.

He was a builder and had done a hell of a lot of work improving our new home, at 147 Lower Paddock Road in Bushey, Hertfordshire. My room was in the loft. Dad had converted it especially for me, all wood panelled and reached by its own ladder from the second floor. I was proud of that room and so grateful he had taken all that trouble just for me. I never wanted to let him down.

I was about twelve when this picture was taken, and already keen on shooting.

He had his office in the house. Nobody else was supposed to enter but we did go in occasionally for odds and sods and one day I went in, I picked up what I wanted – and hesitated, for some reason. I can see it now, that wooden desk, and it still sends a shiver down my back when I remember what I did next. I opened one of the drawers.

It was stacked full of money. Loads of money, dough like I'd never seen. Around £5,000 or more, I reckon, all in banknotes. I closed the drawer and tried to forget about it but it played on my mind. All my life I've had this thing about carrying an angel on one shoulder and a devil on the other. That was where it started. One would be saying to me, 'No, don't touch it,' and the other would contradict: 'Go on … all that money, no one would ever know.'

I regret to this day that I gave in to the little bugger who kept urging me to help myself. But I took one note, a tenner, right from the middle of one of the piles. Can you imagine what that must have been like – a tenner to a seven-year-old? It felt like £100,000. But the crazy thing is that I didn't nick it for myself – and that was my downfall.

I took all my mates down to the sweet shop, but instead of buying penny chews and stuff like that, I bought the whole box. I bought them penknives and all sorts of presents for a couple of days until the money ran out. So I just went back for more, more notes taken from the middle of other piles. The game was up, though, the day one of the teachers at Oxhey Infants School raised the question of little Jones's generosity and how he was coming by the money for the gifts spread around the classroom. I told her my mum and dad knew about the money but I froze on the spot when she called my bluff and said: 'All right, then let's go home and talk to them about it.'

I don't think any statement from anybody has ever frightened me more than that one. I went cold and hot and cold again. My first

thought was 'Oh no, how do I get out of this?' But I knew I was in it, right in it up to my little neck, and deserved everything that was coming my way. When we reached Lower Paddock Road, a scene that would now look as if it came straight out of The Bill greeted us.

As we got out of the teacher's car, my mum, Glenda, was just stepping out of the house. There was another car parked nearby and although it was unmarked I knew by some kind of instinct where it was from. At that age you feared getting on the wrong side of the police.

Mum must have thought I'd been brought home to talk about some routine thing at school because she told the teacher: 'We haven't time for this. We've been robbed. The fingerprint experts are here.' My parents had discovered some of the money had walked from Dad's desk and they'd called the police.

'Well, that's what we're here for,' said the teacher. I was a tiny lad for my age and, right then, as I stood by her side, I was trying to look smaller by the second.

'What on earth do you mean?'

Mum shot a glance from the teacher to me and back again. 'Vinnie's coming to school with all this money in his pocket.'

Mum was a proper mum – one who cared and who put discipline high on her list of priorities. She'd sometimes clipped me round the backside when I'd done wrong and it's strange, now, recalling how Dad used to take her to task for it. This time was different. What I'd done was more serious than a prank and she stuck me in that beloved bedroom of mine, not only while things cooled off downstairs but to wait until Dad came home from work. I sat there stewing and hating what I'd done. But never in a million years did I think he would hit me, because he never had before.

My stomach churned when I heard his voice downstairs. He went absolutely ballistic. He was completely appalled. He gave me such a hiding – only with his hand, but it was a hiding all the same, and I think the shock of it had more effect than the hurt. It really brought home to me what I'd done and it made me ashamed of myself for a long time. It certainly cured me of theft – I could never have turned into a bank robber after that! It didn't end with the hiding, either. He grounded me for the entire summer. It all had a profound effect on me. My isolation forced me to think. I had always regarded myself as a strong kid but I'd given in to the wrong voice from the shoulder. What troubled me most was that I'd let my mum and dad down so badly.

To make things worse, at about the same time, my sister, Ann, who was three years younger than me, needed a bone-marrow transplant. It was an extremely difficult period for my parents. 'How could I have done such a thing?' I asked myself over and over in that bedroom I treasured, during the hours I spent alone.

I have never knowingly taken anybody's property since and never could. I had learned one extremely important lesson. Other lessons have taken longer. I know I hurt my parents deeply but they, without intending to, were to hurt me a few years later at what was the most traumatic time of my life. I've worked bloody hard to make something of myself, but I'll leave you to be the judge.

Chapter 2

The First Shot

My life has been full of ironies, premonitions, coincidences – call them what you like. It all began for me on 5 January 1965 when Vincent Peter Jones took his first breath in Shrodells Hospital. If I'd been tall enough to peep through the window, my first view would have been of nearby Vicarage Road, home of Watford Football Club who, years later, rejected me, saying, among other things, I wasn't big enough to be a footballer.

When you think back to your childhood the memories are black and white, good or bad, happy or sad and there doesn't seem to be anything much in between. My early days must have been a bit cramped as my folks and I shared a house in Queen's Road, Watford, with another family – two rooms, shared bathroom and shared kitchen. And how is this for coincidence? Years later I discovered that Joe Kinnear, my gaffer at Wimbledon, owned half of Queen's Road, including that first house of ours. He also had The One Bell in St Alban's Road, the pub where my mum and her current husband trained as publicans and which they were eventually to take over. And my sister went to the same school as Joe.

The first house I actually remember was in Coldharbour Lane,

A cheeky little monkey.

Watford. I suppose I was about three years old. We had shared accommodation again, rented from the bloke who lived there. There were two other members of the 'family' by then: Titchy and Perky, a couple of Jack Russells, the first dogs we had but by no means the last. I've been living with them ever since. Titchy was the male, all white, and the first character to teach me the meaning of panic. He used to bugger off on regular occasions and we'd spend hours looking for him.

My dad had started out in the heating and plumbing trade and was striving to work his way up. He was such a workaholic that it had cost him a whole string of his mates because while they were out doing what blokes do, drinking and chasing crumpet, he was grafting to get the business going. Parties and the like didn't appeal to him. He was into his shooting and fishing – the interests he had followed from a young age. Shooting was his passion and it became mine as well. The great outdoors has had a terrific influence on my life, so much so that, even in recent years when I've known real success, I have often thought I would have given it all up, forfeited the lot, just to be a gamekeeper.

Dad had built a pigeon hide and you can't begin to imagine the excitement, the wide-eyed wonder of a five-year-old being taken by his father into that secret little place – all netting and camouflage and 'Don't say a word or make the slightest noise.' If I think about it long enough, I still tremble with the anticipation, the tension, the thrill of that first time sitting in the hide with the old man and the gun at the ready. Brilliant!

We had decoy pigeons set out on the ground in front of us attracting the real birds to come down and feed. Dad whispered, 'When one of them sits, boy, you fire.' We had a flask with us. I was on a stool, he had his shooting stick and we were enjoying a cup of coffee. As we looked up, a pigeon came curving in and landed. This was it. Dad rested the twelve-bore on the ledge of the hide. I knew what to do next because he'd talked to me about guns, using them and the respect I must have for them, as he sat and cleaned them in the kitchen.

He helped me position my body properly around the gun and I took aim … squeezed the trigger … Boom! I flew backwards off the stool and the coffee went everywhere, but it wouldn't have mattered even if it had been scalding. 'Have I got it, have I got it?' I was

On holiday in Ireland: I was eleven and Ann eight.

screaming and Dad was crying with laughter. I'd got it!

Mum had been a nurse, but when I was born, that was the end of her working days outside the house until my sister Ann and I were older. She was the one who brought us up, mainly, because she was always around. Ann was born after our move to a council house in Newhouse Crescent, Garston, on the edges of Watford. The house had bushes outside, with big mauve flowers that attracted butterflies by the score. That was another part of life as a kid, and the joy of it, catching butterflies, all shapes and sizes and fantastic colours. There don't seem to be as many nowadays and that should bother us.

I'd started kicking a ball, the way five- or six-year-olds do, and I was always competitive, always wanting to be top man at every activity, and it was the same with butterflies. I spent hours trapping them with my little fishing net when they settled on the flowers and sometimes plucking them out of mid-air. They were the real catches, the ones you made when they were in flight, because that took skill. We kept them in jam jars long enough to judge which kid had caught the most before releasing them. I remember always wanting to be the one with the fullest jar yet getting as much pleasure from letting them go as from catching them in the first place. Some of

the other kids would get bored after a while and go off on their bikes but I'd stay there, catching more.

I don't recall any television sets. Everyone lived in each other's houses. It was kind of communal living for kids, house to house, just turn up and sit down and join in. All the houses were in a row with alleys in between. You went out of your front door, down the alley and you were straight into somebody else's garden. Their bikes and scooters and other toys and even their dogs all muddled up together and we all used to share.

We had a policeman, PC Parkinson, a big man with glasses. He lived on the corner and he and his wife had a couple of girls and a boy. I'd go round there virtually

Ann and me taking part in a talent competition at Warner's Holiday Camp.

whenever I wanted. Over the fence and into their house and I'd end up having tea with them. I was mental for boiled eggs and PC Parky's wife did me them all the time – with soldiers. I was little and hyperactive, never still, but easy and comfortable in anybody's company. I was never put off, scared or even wary of the policeman on the corner of our street. As long as PC Parkinson's wife had eggs in the fridge, he was all right by me.

* * *

I was even more 'all right' after the next transfer of the Jones family to the house in Lower Paddock Road, where from our gate only a small road separated us from the recreation ground.

There were lights all along the road that bordered the 'rec' so we could play football at any time because we had our own 'floodlights' financed by the local council. Eight o'clock was my 'in time', when Mum or Dad used to come out and make the dreaded call that took me from the mates who were allowed to play longer: 'Vin–cent!' I was always thankful that I wasn't the first to have to leave, as there was a bit of a stigma about that. It was an Irish lad, Timothy, who had to go in at 7pm.

Our life was dominated by football. And when my dad brought me back my first proper ball, from holiday in Rimini, well, I was king. Black and white, and genuine leather. None of the other kids could believe it. It was as if something had dropped to earth from Mars and landed in our street. I felt proud and privileged and special, the envy of the area. All the lads, 'Bird' – Peter Burder, my first best mate – Tim and Ray, couldn't bring themselves to play with it at first, because of the thought of getting it scratched, removing that lovely new look that lasts only until the first time you make it meet its purpose. For ages we used it for nothing more damaging than a goalpost. We just sat around it and stared at it. But somebody nicked it. My pride and joy was lifted out of our back garden where the big hedge stretched all the way round to the pub car park next door.

My first school photo – aged five.

We never got it back and whoever stole it ought to know that they left a little lad and his pals heartbroken.

My first real game of football was at Oxhey Infants, nothing grander than one class against another during a PE lesson but your first competitive match is the one you never forget. Having no boots of my own I went to the school's 'Lost and Found' and found a pair. They were white Alan Ball boots, and advertised as used by our World Cup winner of '66. What a stroke of luck, what a find! No matter they were slightly on the big side, I was in business. I also did Bally proud because we won the game and I scored a hat trick, with one of my goals perfectly steered through the goalkeeper's legs.

* * *

Strange things can occur in the mind of a child and something horrible occurred in mine when I was about seven. I had a real panic attack when it first dawned on me that, eventually, everybody dies. Maybe it was because I was having such a great time that this thing about dying had such an awful effect. I couldn't sleep. It was a genuine feeling of panic. I cried almost nightly, wanting my mum to be able to tell me I wouldn't die, wondering where and when I was going to die and have this wonderful life and all the good times taken away from me. I have to admit that, although I don't really know where this phobia came from, I still suffer from it quite a bit, even now – though as I grew older, the fear calmed down and I can control it.

I also went through a terrible time when the family decided to move on, to 'Woodlands', a bungalow dad had bought at Bedmond, near Hemel Hempstead. He was intending to improve it over the years and it was perfect for our shared love of the country, being just off a little lane with about three-quarters of an acre of land. There was a wood to one side of the house, and at the back and round the other side were disused gravel pits that attracted the local youngsters.

The trouble was I couldn't come to terms with leaving Bushey and Lower Paddock Road. I was nine. All my mates and my football were there, in that familiar patch. It was my empire. It was me. I thought that the more I played up the more chance there was of the family deciding to stay put, so I went berserk. I slashed all the

curtains and bedspreads in Mum and Dad's bedroom and in mine, and the front-room curtains as well. Mum and Dad tried to explain that whatever I did would make no difference, but the more they tried to calm me, the more I screamed and cried. I reckon I'm tribal, then as now. For instance, if my wife Tanya suggests going for an evening meal together, the party will have stretched to six people within minutes. I find it very hard to go for a meal, just Tanya and me, even though we are an extremely close couple.

Then one of those weird happenings occurred in the middle of all the turmoil. We were half packed; a lot of the furniture and larger items had gone and the rest was being moved on the Saturday. I looked round the place where I'd been so happy and it was like a ghost house. That night, I had a dream.

Bear in mind I knew nothing of the new place and its surroundings. I think I'd been there once when Mum and Dad were considering buying but I didn't want to know, and I can't remember giving that bungalow a second glance. But I dreamed of a place where I walked up a lane with no one around, crossed a big main road and walked round a council estate with little walls. Round the corner and down a narrow lane and there it was on the left: a football pitch. A green chain-link fence all down one side and the gap where you walked through had a single concrete bollard with a round top. I walked through the gap to the clubhouse and saw, across the pitch, a hedge and goalposts beyond. I saw all that, in the clearest detail, in the dream.

We moved the next day and I had a strange feeling that I was being led and told not to worry, that everything would be all right and my life would resume where it had left off.

When we got to the new place, everybody was busy unpacking and my dad said to me: 'Go into the village, son. Go round the estate and meet the lads.' So off I went: up the lane with no one around, across the main Bedmond Road, past the little walls on the estate, round the corner and down Tom's Lane. By then I knew what I was going to find: the football pitch on the left, the green chain-link fence, the single bollard with the round top, the clubhouse, the hedge and the goalposts beyond – the posts on the pitch at my new school.

I can't account for all that. Nowadays I still look back and see it all twice – first the dream and then how it was in reality. I headed back to the bungalow and it was like darting through a maze. I was thinking on the run, contradictory thoughts. 'I shouldn't be here at all, this is too scary.' And then 'Yes, I should be, it was planned, it was meant to happen.' The way my life has turned out, I am convinced that that house move was intended somehow. The whole area proved to be football crazy.

As for that hedge beyond the football pitch … a couple of years later a professional footballer came to coach us. He had us all chipping the ball over that hedge. He pointed in my direction and said to John Cornell, the bloke in charge of us: 'That boy is head and shoulders above the rest. Let me know how he gets on.'

That footballer was Dave 'Harry' Bassett, the man who signed me for Wimbledon and gave me the chance of a career in the professional game, the man who has had an enormous influence and effect on my life. See what I mean about premonitions and coincidences? Weird.

The dream house, Woodlands, where my childhood happiness fell apart.

Chapter 3

A Fight for Recognition

I wasn't to know it or appreciate it immediately, but it was here in Bedmond and at Woodlands that my life really began, where my passions for football and the country life blossomed until, for a wonderful few years, I thought I'd arrived in paradise. But I had to endure some setbacks along the way: I had to 'qualify'. That process began within minutes of turning my back on the football ground I had seen in my dream.

I was so unnerved by it, so confused and unsure whether it was a good thing or a bad omen that I set off running back to the house where the family's future was being unpacked from cases and boxes. I came to a kind of green where a group of local lads were playing football, so I stopped and watched. The inquisitive banter started and I was suddenly made to realise what it was like to be the new kid on the block. I suppose I'd been looking on and joining in the verbal to-ing and fro-ing for about half an hour when it all 'went off' and a fight broke out. Three of us, all banging away swinging fists and feet. It was two against one with another kid just watching but it wasn't deadly serious. They were testing me out, seeing what the new kid in the neighbourhood was made of. For my part, I was proving to them that the Jones boy was not to be messed around or taken for granted. I think it was the need to be accepted that meant I couldn't afford to give an inch. I can't remember which of us looked worst when it all calmed down, but I came out of it all right. In fact, I came out of it with three new pals – Cal Jenkins, Seamus Byrne and his brother Fran. Cal and Seamus have become lifelong mates – in fact I was best man at Cal's wedding.

School was the next problem. It was all a bit much for a little lad who hadn't wanted to move in the first place, finding himself in a strange house on the Saturday and at a new school on the Monday morning. I'd been at Bedmond Juniors less than a week when my parents were called. I'd been threatening to hurl bricks through the windows and had told one teacher that I wouldn't be at this school much longer because I was going to burn it down.

The headmaster, Derek Heasman, took my dad to one side and told him: 'Mr Jones, I'm worried I've inherited a nutcase.' Or words to that effect. Dad did his best to explain the situation. 'Right, leave it to me. I fully understand the boy's problem,' Mr Heasman reassured him.

'Does he like sport?'

'Crackers about it. Well, mad on football.'

As it turned out, Mr Heasman was a fanatical Queens Park Rangers supporter – he even had the school team turn out in QPR's blue and white hoops. He was also the best PE master you could ever wish for and it's a good job for me that he was. In PE lessons Mr Heasman and I would take on the rest of the class – about fourteen or fifteen others. We had a lad in goal but just he and I as outfield players and I don't recall us ever losing a game. I learned from him how to pass and move properly. I must have learned quickly as well because he put me in the school football team at nine. I'm still the youngest ever to play for that school team. Just as I'm still the youngest to play for the Bedmond first team in the Herts County League.

I was always in trouble in the Juniors,

forever involved in fights for one reason or another, and being sent to Heasman's office for the familiar punishment: whack across the arse with a white plimsoll. With laces. The first time Heasman did it I yelled at him: 'Right, I'm telling my dad and he'll come up here and kill you.' Dad went to the school all right but told Heasman: 'Well done. Do it any time you like.'

I wasn't interested in anything at school if it wasn't connected with sport, although I did quite like drawing. But there was one small thing that persuaded this hyperactive little so-and-so to sit down and sit still. The half-hour storytime in the library. I was transfixed by that brilliant Roald Dahl tale *Charlie and the Chocolate Factory*. I'd sit there hanging on every word. It is the only book that has ever fascinated me. To me it wasn't a story at all; it was absolutely real. I went through a pretty lengthy spell of good behaviour at the time because I knew that if I stepped out of line I'd miss the next reading. It still gives me a good feeling inside when I think about it. I always wanted to be Charlie.

The local estate was where most of my mates lived. Only a couple of us were 'outsiders'. Basically we all belonged in a nice little patch: the council estate, the school, the football pitch and that was us. All tucked into an area so everybody knew everybody and that suited me perfectly. I was known by the kids as a good little scrapper but I was regarded even more highly for my football.

I might have been small but I was ahead for my age in terms of ability. I think it stemmed from the time at Lower Paddock Road where all the others were older than me and I had to try and reach their level. I was strong, I was quick and I could pass the ball. You can watch a team of Under-10s, compare them with a side of Under-14s and the difference is obvious. The younger ones all tend to kick the ball and chase after it. I was different – I could control it, dribble round people and ping an accurate pass, short or long. I wasn't dirty – I couldn't afford to be against bigger lads – but I learned how to look after myself.

So when my dad and a couple of the other dads got together and formed a Sunday-morning side, I turned out for the older team. It wasn't long before people from Watford, Hemel Hempstead and the like had all heard of Vince Jones, the lad in the Bedmond team. By the time I was thirteen or fourteen, I was doing things that blokes of eighteen or twenty were trying, like chipping the keeper from the edge of the box.

Proud moments? None more so, I suppose, than winning the first of the medals that now sit proudly in the cabinet at my home. A match was arranged against Garston boys, a village about five miles

Not quite the model pupil – aged fifteen.

I was only ever
interested in sport,
especially football…

down the road. They arrived along with a big video camera. I still
feel a little glow inside when I think about that day – being presented with the man of the match medal at the age of about nine. It's
only plastic and I've lost the little base it stood on, but it's right there
next to my FA Cup-winner's medal.

From then on, they all wanted me to play for them but I stuck
with the boys from our patch all the way through. For the next few
years I'd usually play games twice a day at weekends, for the school
or the various Bedmond Sports and Social Club teams, beginning
with the Under-10s. The guy who really got us going was John
Cornell, whose son, Jimmy, played as well. John ended up as

manager of Bedmond. When I was about eleven he taught me three tricks.

'Three tips for you, boy,' he said. 'When you knock an opponent over, go and pick him up, be all matey and smile. Pick him up and pull under his armpits at the same time, because the others are all older than you, and when they squeal just act all innocent. When a ball goes through to their keeper and he's standing there with it just run up to him and knock it out of his hand.

'And the third one, if you are being marked too closely just reach back, grab him by the balls and twist. They won't mark you too close next time.' Yes, that's where the incident with Paul Gascoigne shown in that famous photo originated. John wasn't teaching me to cheat. I can see now that he was only suggesting how I could protect myself because I was a small lad competing with much bigger, older players.

Eventually, like many I played with and against, we were chosen for Watford Boys and trained after school at Vicarage Road on Mondays and at Watford Leisure Centre on Thursdays. When I signed the blue schoolboy forms for Watford at the age of twelve Graham Taylor was manager. As you might imagine, I was chuffed. But, I stuck with Bedmond and my old mates – I've always been one to stay with his roots. There was a kids' Sunday team, Ember Echoes, whose manager went round recruiting the best players in the area. It didn't matter how many times he tried to tempt me, I stayed with Bedmond where my old man was manager of the Under-12s.

These really were idyllic times. The disused gravel pits by our house attracted local kids like bees to a honey jar. I have fabulous memories of warm, summer days building rafts, shooting snakes with our air rifles and catapults. And in winter, when it all froze over, ice-skating.

Bird's-nesting was another favourite pastime – great fun, with real excitement finding the nest and identifying the different types of egg. I wonder if youngsters nowadays ever discover the fascination of all that outdoor stuff. Sometimes there'd be thirty or forty of us playing tag in Beechwood Forest. A simple enough little game by normal standards but there was nothing normal about the way we did things. We played tag in the treetops – great big trees. Boys and girls alike, leaping like monkeys from tree to tree and you weren't allowed to touch the ground. What a time we had!

While Dad was into shooting in a big way, Mum preferred bingo. Her only involvement was cooking for the shoot dinners – she didn't know one end of a gun from the other. Dad rented some land and put pheasants down. He was what they called the shoot captain for a syndicate based near St Albans and on a Saturday morning, in the holidays, a group of us would go beating for him. We were paid about £3 apiece which was really good money then. And at the end of the day, as dusk crept in, the men all went on to the duck shoot and took us with them. Wildlife was a great fascination to me. Some of us spent hours with a budgie cage baited with nuts, holding the spring door open with a long piece of cotton. Once a squirrel or a bird was tempted inside you'd release the cotton and trap them. Nothing sinister – we just tagged them and let them go.

But I can't say I'm proud of some of my antics as a nipper when Dad wasn't around. It horrifies me, now, to think of some of the dreadfully cruel things we got up to. Sometimes we took the chickens to Cal's house where there was a wall and a see-saw. We'd put the chicken on one end of the see-saw, then one of us would jump on to the other end off the wall. Not a simple manoeuvre, this. The timing had to be immaculate, not only by the one jumping off the wall but the one letting go of the bird on the see-saw. They were the highest-flying chickens you're ever likely to see. But we soon packed that in. It must have struck even two tearaways like us as cruelty beyond all reason.

We played tricks on other people, too.

Around that time the skinhead fashion was in and a crowd of us often gathered outside the church hall waiting for the old ladies to emerge from bingo. They obviously thought the worst of us, because of how we looked, and I was usually the chosen victim of a mock good hiding as the lads waded in, leaving me spreadeagled on the floor. In came the old girls, flailing their handbags as the boys scattered. 'Are you all right, love?' they'd say to me, crouching down, really concerned. They were not amused when I staged a miraculous recovery, laughed and ran off to join the rest.

By the time I moved on to secondary school at Langleybury half my mates, including Seamus and Cal, were with me and the other half went to another school, Francis Coombe. They lined up on the

Before a game for my dad's side against a team from Merseyside.

opposite side of the road to us as we all waited for the school bus. Two of my best mates were Mark and Paul Robins – like brothers to me, they were. They went to Francis Coombe, so every now and again I went to school with Mark and Paul, explaining to the teacher that I was their cousin, just visiting. No problem – I sat in on the lessons and the school didn't have a clue. I even played for their football team once!

I had two tasks to carry out at home. One was filling up the coal-bunker for the boiler, which meant going down to the bottom of the garden behind the barn in the pitch black. Then on Fridays I had to clean out the dogs' kennels. These jobs had to be done without fail. Work, proper work, found its way on to my agenda when I was twelve or thirteen and Dad set me to work in the building game during the school holidays. I hated it, but I worked for five days a week, with my own timesheet, and Dad handed me my money in cash. I remember wishing he'd give it to me in a proper wage packet like the other builders. I might have hated working but I felt a bit special going down to the youth club with fifteen quid while the others had only about two pounds pocket money. It was Dad's attempt to keep me on the straight and narrow. I was never in really serious trouble, though, no nicking cars or burglary or that kind of stuff. Pranks, basically, fights and generally pissing people off, I suppose. Occasionally there'd be a copper at the door but usually it was someone's mum or dad. If something had gone wrong or something had gone missing, Cal, Seamus or I were the first suspects.

I earned a bit more some Saturdays at the builders' yard in Garston, owned by Russell Hensard's dad, Colin. Russell is another lifelong friend – you will lose count of them by the end of this book. Colin had his own greyhounds and took us to the races at Wembley, Henlow, Walthamstow and such. All the kids loved Russ's dad because he was so generous. As we walked to the greyhound track he would give me a fiver to have a bet. We went along to watch him play Sunday cricket and it was there that I first set eyes on Tanya, now my wife. She was watching the cricket with another family.

I had Sunday dinner with Mark and Paul Robins on a regular basis and if I was out in the estate feeling hungry, rather than get back to my house I was straight round to 'Auntie Chris's' – I still call her that – and Basil's. I'd just walk in the back door, shout 'Is there anything to eat?' grab a handful of biscuits and be off. Or I'd go round with Paul and Mark and Auntie Chris would say, 'Put the kettle on and make us one of your nice cups of tea.' There was a real sense of community, a feeling of warmth, everywhere.

I went back home for a bath and bed, basically. My mum, apparently, was forever asking, 'Where's Vince?' but she knew I'd be safe. Perhaps my staying elsewhere so often had something to do with the half-mile lane that led to our bungalow. The trees on either side met overhead in some places so it was like being in a long, dark cave or tunnel. And if I didn't have my bike with me, I ran.

I learned how to fight, one-handed.

We had one pair of boxing gloves between the lot of us and made a ring area by putting our jumpers down in a circle. You were allowed two rounds, three minutes with the glove on one hand and three more with it on the other, and you could hit only with the gloved hand. I'm not sure what it taught us, exactly, apart from how to get maximum use from the minimum of equipment!

It was going to secondary school that began to open up my life. We played football every single day, always with my ball. I don't know whether it was a case of leadership potential showing itself early, but even in my first year they all came to me to get the match set up – even the fifth-formers, and there were some tough nuts among them, believe me. There was a lad called Dave May who eventually died, tragically, as a teenager with some other friends roaring about in a motor that hit a bridge. He was taken on Chelsea's books at one stage. I loved him. He lived in a council home and he was a right wheeler-dealer, into this and that, a real rogue but get him playing football and he seemed to change character. He was a few years older than me and, like the other lads from the care homes, was regarded as a hard case. But even they would run up to me and plead: 'Give us a game. Where do you want us? Which side are we on?'

I had started watching big-time football with my pal Russ. He was an Arsenal fan and my team was Tottenham so we alternated between the two. It didn't last long, though. One day on the Underground we were confronted by a bunch of lads waving knives. Once was enough – we didn't go again after that.

Chapter 4

What Happened to Paradise?

You're always comfortable as a kid providing you have a routine and it is not disturbed. But when I was thirteen my world caved in. Nothing and nobody can prepare a child for what was about to happen to me at a time when I thought everything in life was just wonderful.

I'd never heard my mum and dad have a row or much of a difference at all. I thought my secure home life would just go on for ever and ever. You learned about other parents splitting up but never expected such things to happen in your own family. At that age, the thought of your parents divorcing seemed as horrifying as if one of them had died. Then the impossible dilemma of having to choose between them – how could a thirteen-year-old properly solve something like that? But it was something I was going to have to face, because the arguments started and went on and on for about a year. I retreated to the comfort of my room, my sanctuary, but there was no escape from the raised voices downstairs. I can still hear Dad's voice to this day, protesting over and over: 'It was a one-night stand, nothing more. And I'm sorry. It wasn't love, it was lust and it doesn't mean a thing.' The proverbial had hit the fan, right out of the blue, when a woman had appeared without warning and knocked at our door. Apparently as soon as Mum answered it the woman came out with the lot: 'I'm getting married but first I want to clear my conscience, get this off my chest, wipe the slate clean. I slept with Peter ten years ago. Just the once, just a one-night stand, but I had to tell you.'

Wouldn't you have thought, after ten years, she'd have let sleeping dogs lie? Maybe she would have done if she'd known the trouble and the heartbreak she was causing us. Dad had made just one mistake, that's all, but little did he know what lay in store as he arrived home from work whistling, happy as a sandboy. Until Mum met him at the door.

Mum and my sister Ann can be quite hard in certain circumstances whereas Dad and I are pretty forgiving. If something upsets us we react full blast at first, but time is a healer with us. With Mum, certainly in those days, it wasn't. The rows between my parents seemed to flare up whenever they were face to face and they got more intense. It makes me shudder when I think of all that stuff, them going at it hammer and tongs, Ann and me cringing upstairs trying not to listen, wanting to shut it out but knowing it was hopeless.

I'd go into Ann's room. I felt that it was up to me to protect her. I'd never had much time for her before. In fact, we fought like cat and dog. Suddenly, though, I felt like the big elder brother. I sat in her bedroom and cuddled her and tried to reassure her as the arguments blazed away downstairs. Sometimes I found myself on the stairs, torn, not sure whether to charge down and grab hold of my mum or dad, or run and take hold of my sister. I suppose I was crying out for Ann to cuddle me as well. We never really bonded until later on in our lives but at that troubled time we shared a dreadful feeling of insecurity, made worse by the fact that Mum was now sleeping upstairs and Dad downstairs.

It was a good thing when Mum eventually left, even though the timing was a bit unfortunate: the day before my fourteenth birthday. We were back from school when she came in with her black bag, knowing my dad was at work, and gathered together all her things. I was clinging on, both arms wrapped around her legs, begging her not to go. She was trying to explain why she had to but she wasn't herself. It's a bit of a blurred picture, that awful scene, but I remember vaguely that she had people with her, and I yelled at them: 'Fuck off! Leave my mum alone. Get out of our house!' It was no good, though. Finally I had to let go.

* * *

Because of the trouble at home, my prospects of a career with Watford Football Club were put in doubt. Mum picked me up from school and dropped me off wherever Watford Boys were training, but afterwards I had a half-hour walk to the station, and had a good four-mile walk from the station to the bungalow at nine or ten o'clock at night. When things were fine at home, it was no sacrifice at all. I would have done anything to go training with a proper club. But I had begun to miss training sessions here and there. I could feel things slipping a bit because I was often so tired, having sat up until the early hours listening to the arguing.

You are never properly prepared for bad news even if you half expect it, and that's how it was when they kicked me out of Watford. For the first time, I was told I wasn't good enough. On decision day as to who would be taken on and who would be released, all the other lads went in one by one, but they called in my best mate Graham Coles and me together.

Bertie Mee, the former Arsenal manager whose team did the League and FA Cup Double in 1971, had overall responsibility for the youth set-up. He was clutching his folder. What happened next was what all starry-eyed, would-be future stars dread most: that shattering moment that says the pro game, or at least this pro club, doesn't want you. Bertie peered over his glasses but didn't say anything for a second or two. I was praying he'd get it over with. At last he said, 'We have decided, rightly or wrongly, that we are going to release you both from your schoolboy forms at Watford. We are not going to take you on as apprentices.' He explained to Colesy first: 'Graham, we think we are making a mistake with you. It was very close, we've spoken to various coaches but decided to release you although we appreciate we may be making an error.' Colesy was a midfield player, tucked in behind the front two, or a winger. A bit of a Peter Beardsley you might say. But all was not lost, Bertie assured him. West Brom, Coventry and Leicester were interested.

Then he turned to me. 'Vinnie, you treat life as one big joke.

Unfortunately, we think you are going to be too small. Nothing wrong with your football, your ability, but your size is a problem. We've retained other boys ahead of you because of your height.' I couldn't take that in. I thought that if you could play, you could play. Size shouldn't come into it. But Watford seemed to have a thing about it. My dad had been told a fair time earlier that I needed to fill out, that he should give me a bottle of Guinness or Mackeson each dinnertime and make me sit for half an hour to absorb it properly. No chance and my dad knew it. After every meal I was out with a ball in the back garden on my own, or out with the lads.

But dear old Bertie tried to soften the blow with me as well, saying I had the chance to go to Coventry, like Colesy, and that Tottenham had also shown an interest. I didn't bother with either. It didn't seem to matter as much as before. Colesy went to West Brom but hurt his ankle in training and nothing materialised. We both had a spell over at Hertford Town, but it seemed miles to travel so we packed it in and went our separate ways.

If Mum and Dad had been together, maybe I would have pursued the so-called 'interest' from a couple of clubs. But Dad had started to see another woman, and was still trying to run a business and the shoot, and there were continuing problems with my mum. If it hadn't been like that, I'm sure he'd have said, 'Right, let's get those numbers and we'll take you training.'

Worse was to come. I was to lose everything with the split at home. Not only my family and my football dream world at Watford but my close friends as well because, to give Mum her share of the money, my dad was forced to sell the beautiful house he had worked like hell to get just right.

Dad, my sister and I moved into an old, semi-detached, labourer's house he bought from a farmer in Colney Heath, St Albans, and Mum took a job in a nursing-home where she lived in. My life had been building up nicely, brick by brick, but now it felt like a bulldozer had driven straight through it.

Like any kid in his early teens, I needed my mates, and in the circumstances I needed that feeling of belonging even more than ever. The move to Colney Heath meant that Ann and I had to go to a new school – Chancellors' in Brookmans Park. I felt I was good for nothing. My mates were living over near Watford and I was on the other side of St Albans. Gone, the lot.

After I'd been at the school for about six weeks I'd had enough of the place. I didn't really know anyone and I was desolate. I did manage to get on with a couple of lads, but I didn't give a toss about anything much, apart from biology which I quite liked and did have a bit of a go at it. I was interested in evolution, how things were formed, the development of the bird from the egg, and so on. It was the only thing that held my interest. I'd even stopped playing football at break times.

I didn't tell anyone about my football background, that I was pretty good at it, that I'd played for Watford Boys and the Hertfordshire county side, but after a couple of games during PE other boys started taking notice and urged me to play for the school team. I refused to begin with but relented and played once or twice.

You'd have thought the football might have eased the situation, tempted me back on track, but when the time came when I had to declare which exams I would be taking, it was an easy question for me: 'None. I'm taking no exams. In fact, I'm out of here.' The teachers knew my mind was made up and that there was no point in attempting to change it. They suggested I went to work for my dad, turning the last months of my schooling into a kind of work experience. They released me from Chancellors' and I've still never taken an exam in my life.

Dad had his problems, as you might imagine. He was trying to get his life going again. Not surprisingly, he needed love and comfort and he found it with his new girlfriend. The trouble was there were times when he wasn't home until three or four in the morning, or even the next day. It wasn't his fault; he'd just lost the plot. I never thought, though, that he would find his treasured shoot a burden. Looking back, he must have been on the verge of some sort of breakdown. He passed the shoot to the farmer next door, who he'd bought the house from, and asked him to run the shoot until he could get his head right.

They had a gamekeeper, Neil Robinson, who with his wife Andrea lived in a rented cottage up at the wood. I spent much of my time with them, helping rear the pheasants but, generally, just wanting to be there. They didn't have children of their own and being there I started to feel I had something like a home again.

Mum arrived once a week to take us out. How I hated that. It was all so forced, with so little genuine emotion. I refused to go after a few occasions but Ann felt a bit guilty, I think, and went each week. Ann stayed pretty close to Mum but I didn't have a lot to do with her for some time and when she rang up, I was always busy.

The divorce was terrible, too. There was me, Dad, Nan and my auntie sitting on one side of the room and my Mum and a couple of her mates on the other. Horrible. She knew I wouldn't leave Dad, that my football and shooting would keep us together, but she wanted custody of my sister. Eventually and thankfully Dad pointed out to her that all this was crucifying the kids and about a week after the court hearing she decided not to pursue her custody claim.

Little wonder, then, that school could not sustain my interest and concentration. I had to get out and do something different, so it was off to the building site. Up in the morning at the same time as my dad and away in the van. He dropped me off to join his other blokes building house extensions. Humping bricks in a hod, digging, mixing cement – general builder's labourer, that was me at sixteen.

The old man needed some time off work when his hand went septic, so he gave me the keys to the van and there I was driving all round the Watford area, without a licence. I wasn't old enough to drive. Some days I even took the lorry – anything to keep the firm ticking over while Dad was out of action. I'd be picking up supplies, having a laugh and a crack with the boys, working a fiddle here and there. Ten bags of cement on the back of the truck and they'd bill us for five. I was really enjoying this little lot but if Dad had been sound in his head at the time he would never have let me do it.

Dad met Jenny Ambrose, who is his wife today, and she screwed his head back on and helped him start to get his life back together. Mum met a fella, Dave Hockey, who is now her husband. All of a sudden life started to get better. At least, that's what I thought. We spent the best part of a year building my dad's new house. He had bought some woods off a shoot with planning permission years earlier.

I liked Jenny, liked her a lot, and still do. I accepted her because she was such a lovely person, but I couldn't have anyone else as my mum. She was living at her own house, constantly backwards and forwards between her place and ours, but she didn't stay over. Peace, real peace, rarely seemed to last very long. I started mucking about at the building game to such an extent that Dad told me: 'You'd better go and get a job, son.' When the Youth Opportunities scheme was introduced, Vinnie Jones was one of the first involved. Stacking supermarket shelves at £23.50 a week. Some bloody opportunity!

I started staying overnight at Neil and Andrea's cottage, sometimes because we'd be up all night rabbit shooting or on the lookout for poachers. I think my dad began to resent the fact that I was spending so much time there. Perhaps he sensed that I was looking on Neil as a kind of father figure. I remember the two of them had a blazing row on our doorstep and, in the middle of the argument, with me standing at the kitchen door and yelling at the old man, he spun round and gave me a right-hander. It was the last time I ever went into that house. I went upstairs to my room, gathered together my gear and football medals and stereo and stuffed them into a black bag. I jumped into the Land Rover with Neil and went to his cottage – my life bundled up in a black bin-liner.

I stayed with Neil and Andrea for three or four days. I told him I wanted to get out, to clear off and make a fresh start somewhere. So he rang his father to see if he could get me a job. And he managed it, but not in gamekeeping as an underkeeper or something of that kind, something I longed to do. He got me in at the boys' public school Bradfield College, near Reading. Neil's dad, Tom, was the hairdresser who called at the college a couple of times a week. He went to see the bursar and he got me a job: washing pots and pans!

Tom came from Newbury to pick me up. Me with all my worldly goods in a black bin-bag. I felt lost, alone in a strange, big posh school wondering what the future had in store. Tom went off to cut hair and the bursar took me to my room. I don't even remember dumping the bin-liner in the room before the bursar took me to the kitchens and introduced me to Mick, the head chef. He was tall and clean-looking and turned out to be a really nice old boy. That was it. I was left there with the chef and the two sinks where I was to spend just about all my time.

'You wash the pots and pans,' Mick said to me. 'Wash them, then sterilise them in that tank, dry them and then put them away. I suggest you do it like this.'

He gave me a demonstration and I just stood there, looking and listening. On one side of me were all the racks, crammed with the pans and all the other gear they use in a kitchen. On the other stood a guy called Harry. He was the potato peeler – at least the bloke who cut the spuds in the big machine that peeled them for him. He turned out to be a good pal, Harry – always willing to say, 'Go on, son, you get off and I'll do it' if I needed to shoot off early.

Mick took me back to my room. He told me that the first door on the left was home to a bloke called Reg. He was in his mid to late forties, I'd say, had only one leg and never seemed to leave that room 365 days of the year. Apparently, he had worked as a groundsman or something and there had been an accident involving lime that eventually led to the amputation. The school had looked after him, given him a room with his own little kitchen and bathroom. And that's where he stayed in his wheelchair.

Next door along was the shared bathroom, very basic and with paper peeling off the walls. Out of the bathroom, two steps and into the shared kitchen with its Baby Belling. Opposite the bathroom was Harry the caretaker's room. And a bit further along was John's room – the college maintenance man.

Then mine. It was built on a corner and overlooked the gardens and the sports field, which was lovely, and there was a river at the bottom. It was almost bare – just a bed and bedcovers and a carpet. My wardrobe was outside the room in the corridor. I unpacked my few clothes and then, one by one, took out my football medals and mementoes and set them out on the windowsill and mantelpiece. I put out my stereo and a few records and that was the lot.

I sat on the bed. Suddenly it dawned on me that it was Friday, that I wasn't due to start work until seven o'clock on the Monday morning so I had the whole weekend to get through. It was horrendous. The nearest shop was about three or four miles up the road and I had only a tenner to my name so I opted for an early night, which seemed fine – until all bloody hell broke loose. Harry and John, the two piss artists, went to The Queen's Head, the nearest pub, after work on Fridays and then got stuck into the whisky when they got back to their rooms. That was their weekend: down to the bookies together, into the pub together, back to their rooms and into the Scotch. And spark out on their beds having forgotten all about the beans they'd put on the Baby Belling – burned beyond recall. God knows how I got through that weekend before Neil's dad called and took me to his place for lunch on the Sunday. But however bleak things appear at first, however unfamiliar and frightening, you do adjust. Especially when you have to. Monday morning arrived – down to the kitchen, seven o'clock sharp, and suddenly I was a lot happier, occupied, off and running. And eating properly for the first time in ages.

Boy, did I eat.

It was a great routine. After breakfast for the boys and the masters, we could take our pick of the stuff that hadn't been eaten. I was having four or five boiled eggs in a morning plus the bread rolls that went with them. A big roast at dinnertime, three cracking good meals a day with everything fresh. Washing up three times a day didn't seem such a sacrifice after all. And in the evenings it was off to The Queen's Head. Work done, I'd cadge a lift, stay at the pub all evening then walk home. I was such a regular, killing time at the dartboard, that they put me in the pub team.

They had a football team at the pub, too, but I didn't tell them I played. I didn't want the hassle or the responsibility. Football, then, was something I avoided because if I'd started playing it would have constantly reminded me of what had happened and meant going through it all again. It would also have meant putting myself to the test, trying to rediscover the high standard I'd achieved. Having not played for quite some time I think I was a bit scared of failing. Better just to be known as Vinnie, the bloke who worked at the college, played darts, had a drink at the pub.

I was a bit wary of Reg, but soon realised he was a sweet man and I sort of befriended him. I started doing bits of shopping for him and he'd give me a pound for going. I used to sit with him, just chatting about this and that, what was going on around the college, where I'd come from, what had happened to him. He got to me after a while and I started thinking about how awful it was for a great fella who'd been used to the outdoor life to be confined to one small room all year round. I thought it wasn't right that he was on his own and on the spur of the moment I went out and bought him a budgie and a cage out of my wages. He loved it dearly; in fact it became his life.

The summer break arrived like a win on the pools. The pay in advance amounted to close on £500. My transport problem was solved at a stroke – and at a cost of almost half my sudden windfall – by a beaut of a motorbike, a white 250cc Kawasaki. That was me, then, roaring around Berkshire full blast on my mean machine. No licence, no insurance, no tax – irresponsible, downright bloody crazy, I suppose, looking back, but you did things like that as a youngster. I'd got my left ear pierced by now. It was the latest fashion and I didn't want to feel untrendy. I did it myself in my room at Bradfield. I'd got hold of an ordinary sewing needle – I don't think I sterilised it – and just sat slowly forcing it through my earlobe. I put a poxy little fake stud in the hole and it turned my ear grey and green. I have a £1,000 diamond in it these days.

After the holidays, I didn't mind being back in the old routine with pots and pans for company, twelve hours a day. I was ticking away nicely, being paid, roaring around on my bike and had no shortage of pals. It all changed on one of the little country lanes between college and the village. I was belting along, when suddenly, round one of the bends, there was a great lorry heading for me. I turned the bike, went hurtling up a bank and through a barbed-wire fence. The lorry continued on its way, but I ended up in the college hospital with cuts and a badly injured wrist.

I don't know whether it dawned on me all of a sudden that, despite new friends and what seemed like a pretty good existence, the reality was working long shifts and washing pots and pans. And to top it off, my bike was sabotaged. When Mum turned up, I just said: 'I can't take all this any more.'

She said: 'Come on, collect your gear and we'll get you in the car.'

I packed up, left a note and went.

Mum was still living in at the nursing home and I hadn't spoken to my dad in nine months or more. I used to ring my sister Ann from a phone box and she would nearly always cry even though I always told her I was all right and not to worry about me. I'd sent her a radio-cassette player for her birthday in an attempt to convince her how well I was doing.

The question, on the way from Bradfield, was where to go. Neil and Andrea Robinson no longer worked for Dad. They were game-keeping near Hitchin and Mum took me straight there. I tried to get a job, going to interview after interview wearing Neil's game-keeping gear because I'd never had a suit and tie in my life. Maybe it was a struggle to get work because of the 'vision' I presented at the interviews decked out in Neil's tweed jacket and trousers several sizes too big. I went for jobs at Homebase, B & Q, places like that, answering advertisements for shelf stacking and the like. There'd be twenty other people after the same job and I had only one refer-ence, from Neil.

So I stayed on the dole and worked with Neil as a kind of under-keeper and I loved it. I was me again, doing what I liked most, known and acknowledged by the head gamekeeper, beating for the shoots and generally helping out and hoping that if a genuine job came up on the estate I'd be able to put in for it. If that had happened, it's a reasonable bet that professional football would never have seen Vinnie Jones. I would be a gamekeeper now, with many years' experience.

Not long after I moved in with Neil and Andrea, Cal Jenkins bumped into my mum. They'd had no contact for ages but, of course, he asked about me. He had just passed his driving test and drove over, in his new Escort estate, to see me.

'What are you up to with your life?' he asked. 'We are all into the nightclubs and pubs, having a great time of it.'

'I spend my time watching for poachers, feeding the pheasants, that kind of stuff,' I told Cal and I could see kind of a sympathetic look settle on his face although he didn't actually raise his eyebrows.

'Come and spend the weekend at my house and join the rest of the lads. You'll love it.' With Neil and Andrea's encouragement I went to Cal's home for three or four weekends, and began to get a taste for the night life, seeing my old mates again and getting out and about in Cal's car. I was one of the lads again, nightclubbing and fighting, often running from the police after various bust-ups.

There was another price to pay for my newfound freedom. Things became too much for Andrea and Neil. It wasn't their fault; it was mine. I was changing before their very eyes. No longer up at first light and out tending the pheasants. I was lying in bed. It was hardly surprising that arguments followed. The wanderer was off again, this time to live with Cal.

I was still on the dole, still hadn't spoken to my dad, but I was with familiar faces and that alone gave me a sense of security.

We went into business. Well, the nearest thing to a business we were capable of setting up. There's a big roundabout at Watford called The Dome. We borrowed £25 off Cal's dad, bought six buckets, a long hosepipe and an eight-foot by four-foot sheet of plywood. We painted 'Cal's Car Wash' on it in big letters and stood it on the roundabout. We connected the hose to the water supply at the nearby garage, borrowed a corner of their forecourt and spent the whole summer washing cars. But everything we made, we spent – on the piss in the clubs.

Washing cars every day throughout the summer, wearing Doc

Marten boots and a pair of shorts and lying out in the sun during any spare moments, it was one of the best times of my life. Cal and I knew just about everybody in Watford so they all used our car wash.

On returning home from the garage one evening we found Cal's dad in shock. 'We're at war,' he told us. 'This country's at war.' Cal and I thought it must be World War III, nuclear weapons and all that, but the Falklands became the big talking point as the build-up went on and one night Cal and I decided to join up. We were totally serious about volunteering. We agreed it would be a great idea to put ourselves to some worthwhile use. So we headed for the Army Recruitment Office in Watford and told them we wanted to sign on for the conflict in the Falklands.

'What about this criminal record?' I heard the bloke in charge ask Cal. He'd had to declare on the form that he'd been in court and been convicted for a breach of the peace. Whatever it was, it was enough to wreck our plan. The Army wouldn't accept Cal and we had made a pact that if one of us didn't get in, the other wouldn't join. But we never thought we'd fall at the first bloody hurdle.

You do some daft things at seventeen. We were serious about going to fight a war somewhere in the southern Atlantic because we didn't particularly fancy washing cars in the winter! I reckon one punch-up that found its way on to Cal's record did me one of the biggest favours of my life.

Punch-ups were a regular occurrence,

every Friday and Saturday. We didn't go looking for it but nearly always ended up involved in one – occasionally needing stitches for our trouble. The pattern was familiar – about thirty of us meeting up at The Three Horseshoes in Garston. It was like a religion. Always there by 7pm on the dot and drinking bottles of Skol Special. Loads of people around, acquaintances, girlfriends, strangers.

We'd steam off to another pub. Bosh! Bother! Something would trigger a row and a fight would follow so often that it eventually seemed like normal behaviour. There was always a ruck at The New Penny in Watford, or at Bailey's nightclub. We were fighting all the time. The Friday-night punch-ups were the talk of Saturday afternoon and the Saturday-night punch-ups were the talk of Sunday dinnertime. It went on like that for months and I have to confess that, yeah, I loved it.

Feeding pheasants on Dad's shoot.

Cal's dad, who thought the world of me and still does, was waiting up for me on one occasion after a bit of a 'set-to' with the occupants of a car we'd cut up. As I arrived home he came out brandishing a golf club and yelling: 'There's your bag. Now piss off!' He'd had enough of the late nights, the scraps and the worry. I couldn't blame him. Luckily for me, my Auntie Margaret lived nearby. I just walked round to her house with my worldly possessions, in a green football-kit bag this time, and set up my latest base, on her sofa.

I knew I couldn't exist like that for long so eventually I phoned my mum to explain my latest dilemma. One of her friends, now dead, had a son, Colin Bushby, and she suggested I went to see him. He was a strange bloke in some ways, Colin, single and in his forties, I suppose, but he was brilliant to me. He took me in. He had a two-bedroomed flat in Summerhouse Way, Abbots Langley. I was back near my old patch, less than a couple of miles from Bedmond. As I was still on the dole, I would cook dinner and we'd sit and watch television together.

The lads were urging me to take up football again. I hadn't played since Watford, but I was still eligible to play for Bedmond's Under-18s. My mate Russell Hensard said: 'Listen, Vinnie, the team are crap. We're getting hammered every week. All the boys are involved so why don't you join us?' I thought about it and, well, what would I do with my Wednesday nights otherwise? And it is nice to hear you're wanted. They took me training and made sure the manager, Johnny Moore, was there to see me.

'This is Vinnie Jones and we want him to sign on,' they told him.

'Well, let me have a look at him training first.' Johnny hailed from Rickmansworth, so he didn't know me. He'd only heard that I was a good player. He couldn't believe his eyes, or that's what he said. He wanted me in the team and, somehow, I think I realised the time had come to start doing something with my life. I had wasted time but now my mates had steered me round another corner and made sure I didn't waste everything.

Before long it seemed that every team wanted me and I was playing for the lot. Starting with the Under-18s who, in fact, were the whipping boys for the rest of their league. Soon I was in Bedmond's first team, playing men's football on Sundays, for the Glenn in Watford and St Joseph's from Bushey. I couldn't get enough, all of a sudden, and couldn't understand how I'd managed to get along without the game. The pattern was to play for the reserves on Saturday mornings, the first team in the afternoons, St Joseph's, Glenn or Leggetts on Sunday mornings – three matches each weekend and a midweek game for Bedmond thrown in.

I earned a tenner or so a time by doing some gardening and odd jobs for Johnny Moore. He felt sorry for me and one day, out of the blue, he arrived at Colin's flat with his wife Wendy and their children. Johnny said simply: 'Get all your stuff together. We've had a family meeting at our house and we want you to come and live with us.' Coincidences? I became part of their family living in Tom's Lane, Bedmond, a stone's throw from my previous home. I shared a bedroom with their son, Sean, and we are still close to this day. I regard him as a brother. John and Wendy really are incredible people and Sean and their daughters Debbie, Michelle and Victoria make up what must be the perfect family.

There was a lot of hardship around at that time, no shortage of one-parent families, but if any of the lads from the football team were in danger of going without Sunday dinner they were encouraged to come round to Tom's Lane. Sometimes there would be ten or fifteen of us and everyone loved being there. John and Wendy have never changed and they are still as kind and generous with their time and effort today.

Johnny had lost his father and he kept telling me that it wasn't right for me not to be in contact with my dad. I hadn't seen him for almost three years. Johnny and Wendy kept chipping away, and in the end Cal and I went to see him. It was a difficult meeting, both of us finding it hard to choose the right words. In fact, we just talked about this and that as though nothing had happened. It was reassuring to realise that the separation hadn't done any lasting damage and, nowadays, we couldn't be closer.

Our reunion wasn't exactly blissful to begin with. It wasn't long before Dad had me working back on the building sites, but I was that bit older and wanted to show him that I could stand on my own two feet, so I left to work for other building firms, returned to my dad for a while and then was off to do some labouring for others again – including digging out footings at weekends with a mate of mine, Mark Atwood. It was meeting Mark and becoming such good friends that began a transformation of my life.

Chapter 7

Say a Little Prayer

Mark's dad, Peter, was head groundsman and gardener at the Masonic School in Bushey, the International University of Europe, and he found me a job there. At last, Vincent Peter Jones – hedge pruner, hoer, sweeper-up of leaves – joined the legions of British taxpayers.

Gardening was the worst job in the world in the freezing cold and pouring rain. If I close my eyes, I can see myself clear as day trundling around eighty acres of grounds with a wooden rake, tractor and trailer and the two boards that you used to pick up the leaves. Hour after hour, day after day. But at least it was work.

And I started playing football with the students. Peter had told the sports master I was quite a performer and I was allowed to take Wednesdays off work to turn out for the college football team. One team led to another, and they formed a Sunday side, the IUE Flyers, and would you believe it, we made it into the Watford and District League. It was some team for a Sunday-morning outfit. Mark Atwood and I found ourselves in a side with players from Nigeria and all over the place. Saturday mornings with Bedmond, Sundays with the Flyers – football was growing in importance, dominating

my thoughts. I was basking in my own little bit of glory one after-noon, cutting the grass in front of the large college house on a great big motor mower. I was doing pretty well, one of the youngest ever players to make it to the Bedmond first team, and I had a write-up in the local paper as well for two free kicks against Cockfosters. I made the headline on the match report. Two screamers, both from outside the box, one in each half – wallop, through the laces, top corner.

Lost in my own thoughts suddenly I was praying – a proper prayer. It was to my granddad, Arthur, Dad's father. My prayers were always to him and still are when I find the need. He and Nan were always special. Granddad was kind of head of the family in many ways: his word ruled. He had a walking stick but didn't use it for walking – it meant he could keep everybody in order and give us the odd jab or two if necessary without having to jump out of his armchair.

He died in October 1977 and it had a deep effect on me. It was the first time I'd experienced a death in the family, the suddenness of it, the abruptness and the awful emptiness of the space Granddad used to occupy. How does a kid reach the favourite old man who isn't there any more?

I've always believed he is still in touch. I am convinced he is my spiritual guide. I remember saying out loud: 'I'd love to be a profes-sional footballer, Granddad. Fourth Division, anything. It's a foot-baller I want to be, Granddad. I don't know how we can do it but one chance is all I need. If you can help …'

Maybe it was a week or two later when Alan, the sports master, came over to me in the grounds one morning and said: 'We'll have to get this football pitch in proper shape because Wealdstone are coming to do their pre-season training here.'

Wealdstone! The top boys from the Gola League, now the Conference, with their ex-pros from Fulham and Chelsea and all over. This was a big-time football team to me and they were coming to practise right there where I worked. When their manager, Brian Hall, told me: 'You can join in with us if you like,' there was only one thing to say: 'Thanks, Granddad.'

I soon thought of something that would take the eye, make them notice. It's something I've repeated at every opportunity throughout my career. When it came to the long training runs, cross-country, I told myself: 'Go and win it – it's the one at the front they'll remember most.' It must have worked because I was soon travelling with them to other training venues. Training and travelling, but not playing. Wealdstone's reserve side played in the Capital League where professional clubs like Wimbledon turned out their own reserve teams. I travelled with them for some time, desperate to be a substitute, longing for my chance to prove I could pass the test.

Which brings me to the day of my driving test. I took it at nineteen, borrowing the fee from my mum. I hadn't had a lesson. Well, I'd driven as a kid and used Cal's car a few times in the days of our car wash, and that seemed like experience enough. So I announced it among the boys in the pub: 'I've got my test tomorrow, lads. Anybody lend me a motor?'

Michael Conway, a year or two older than me, answered the distress call: 'My sister-in-law's got a Mini Traveller. I'll give her a buzz.' We had a bond between all of us that somehow seemed to carry a guarantee. Whatever was promised would be carried out.

'Right,' I said, 'I'll meet you down at the test centre in Clarendon Road.' He was as good as his word. And, as you might have guessed, most of the other boys turned up as well. It was quite an event – me taking my driving test with no insurance, no tax, nothing, in a vehicle I'd never seen before, let alone driven. No wonder they promised me: 'If you pass today, we'll all show our arses in Harrods' window.'

In I went. 'Mr Jones.'

'Yes,' I blurted.

'Yes,' came the same reply from somebody else within a split second.

'What?' I said, looking round and feeling a bit of a prat and thinking I'd made my first mistake already. Then this bloke in heavy black-rimmed glasses stepped forward. Mr Jones the examiner.

The Mini Traveller was on the other side of the road as the two of us emerged from the centre to be greeted by the lads sitting on the bonnet giving me the appropriate hand signals. They were still giving it plenty as Mr Jones and Mr Jones pulled slowly and illegally away from the kerb.

The driving itself was no bother, hardly a mistake, as I remember. Then the question. 'Where in the road do you think you should be driving?' I paused for quite a time, half wondering about the question but mostly hoping that the other Mr Jones didn't notice what this Mr Jones already knew – that the tax was out, that right there little more than a foot from the end of his nose was nothing more than a home-made disc insisting that the real disc was 'Applied for'.

'That's a hard one,' was my immediate, brilliant response to his question. 'Where should you drive in the road? In the middle.'

I thought I had blown it because he jumped on my answer. 'What? You mean you should straddle the white line?'

'No, no. I mean you should drive in the middle of your own lane to give enough room to cyclists when overtaking.'

'Mr Jones,' he said. 'I'd like to congratulate you on passing your test. Well done.'

I wanted to yell 'You what?' but controlled the urge until I'd left the car and been greeted by my familiar welcoming party all fearing the worst and totally gobsmacked when I let it out: 'Yeeeaaahhhh!' They all started shouting and we headed straight for the pub. Mikey wouldn't let me drive the car there, but once inside I couldn't hold back: 'Right, you tossers, up to London and let's see your arses in Harrods' window.'

* * *

Patience, all the travelling around, paid off for me when I was given a few reserve games here and there. Nothing spectacular but I gave it everything at every opportunity, training and playing for my life. There were to be many memorable days at Wealdstone but none has stayed with me clearer than the call from Brian Hall, the manager, to tell me: 'You've done brilliantly, you've stuck at it and done well in the Capital League. We want you to be part of the squad now.'

I was a semi-pro, on £28 a week plus the odd £20 to cover expenses now and then. Not only that, but they gave me a club blazer and tie. That was my pride and joy: to be able to wear the official gear. I'd stopped playing for Bedmond's first team after signing for Wealdstone, but I went back every Saturday night with my blazer and tie on and often told a fib, that I'd been substitute when I hadn't. It was nice to hear everybody saying: 'Brilliant, well done, keep it up.'

It was around this time that Mum married Dave Hockey, while Dad got married to Jenny, too. It's nice to be able to say that they are all still together. I continued living at Johnny Moore's and working with Dad in the building game. House extensions, mainly, with me doing the labouring – digging out, loading, mixing cement, hod-carrying. To be honest, there were times when I really bloody hated it – most of the time, come to think of it.

But Dad had caught the football bug again. He was happy to let me go off training a couple of times a week, and he and Jenny started coming to watch me in matches. I was flying – happy to have finally made things up with the old man and really determined to make the most of the big chance that came my way through somebody else's appalling misfortune.

A dreadful thing happened to our first-team centre half, Dennis Byatt from Northampton. He lost his wife and baby during childbirth in hospital. Dennis is another whose friendship I've kept over the years. Who could ever forget that such terrible circumstances offered you the chance to take the first steps of a career? During Dennis's time away from the club I was put in at centre half. It was the season Wealdstone were going for both Gola League and FA Trophy titles – aiming to be the first non-League side to do the Double.

One of my first games was away to Frickley Colliery. What a name that is! There was a fire in the dressing-room with a bucket of coal to keep it going. Outside, beyond the ground, were all those little houses, row after row. It was a night game with a crowd of around a thousand. There was that strange smell in the air that seems to come with fog. We were winning the game 2–0 and the mist was getting worse, so bad that it became difficult to see the Frickley goal.

The home fans clearly didn't like the thought of their side getting beaten and took extreme action. They lit a great fire behind one goal, doubling the effect of the fog that already had us worrying that the game might be abandoned. You could hardly see anyone in the other half of the pitch but the attempted sabotage had the opposite effect because the referee told us: 'Right, that's it. We're going to finish this match now at all costs.' Brilliant! We had vital points in the bag and he refused to call it off, even though at a corner kick in the last couple of minutes we couldn't even see the

geezer taking it. We finished as two-goal winners. It was the first time I ever shook a referee's hand and meant it.

I fixed myself up with a set of wheels: I bought myself a blue Mini Van from a friend for £110. Again, no tax, no insurance, nothing. I used it the night some of us visited a nightclub and volunteered to take a mate home. It was only about ten minutes away by car. My pal Dave Jefferson came with me. On the way back a police car drove past us in the opposite direction along the High Street in Abbots Langley. I glanced in the mirror and saw the car turn round so I put my foot down and shot off. Not because I'd had a load to drink – I'd taken it steady with a few beers because we had a match next day – but I was worried about the lack of tax, insurance and so on.

I turned into a cul-de-sac and saw a big caravan in one of the driveways so I parked behind it and sat there. We were just opposite The King's Head, an old watering hole of ours. We sat for what seemed like ages, probably half an hour or so, rolled a fag and chatted. We could have left the car and walked home in fifteen minutes across the fields. On reflection we should have done exactly that, but we thought we were in the clear. I reversed out of the drive but as we reached the end of the cul-de-sac two police cars eased out of the pub car park. Wallop – they were on me.

It turned out that an electrical shop in Abbots had been turned over – the window caved in and televisions nicked. When the police saw a gash on my foot, I became prime suspect. I've had this thing about socks all my life. I don't wear them, unless I have a suit on or

The Wealdstone squad, with me fifth from right at the back, celebrating our 2–1 victory in the FA Trophy final in 1985.

I'm out shooting. I wasn't wearing any that night and during a bit of aggro at the nightclub a glass had dropped on my foot and cut it. The cops dragged us out of the car, slung Dave into the back of one of their vehicles, handcuffed me and chucked me into the other.

We were taken to Watford nick and they kept us there all night. I was breathalysed and registered 43 on the scale where 35–40 was supposed to be OK. At least, that was my understanding of it. I was later fined and disqualified from driving for eighteen months.

But that night the lads from CID kept coming into the cell and waking us and roughing us up a bit and insisting: 'Come on … tell us.' They were convinced we'd done the electrical shop. I was done for drink-driving and they released me at ten o'clock in the morning. In just one hour, I had to take the bus from Watford to Abbots to pick up my van, then belt to Bedmond for my club blazer and tie and get back to Wealdstone for the coach to the match in Maidstone.

I had no boots so I borrowed a pair from somebody, size nines instead of eights, and one of them flew off into the crowd with my very first kick in the pre-match warm up. I got it back, persevered and we won the game.

Trouble followed me to Gateshead where a fight I got involved in outside a hotel bar was kept quiet from Brian Hall because, only the week before at Maidstone, he'd told me I had to watch myself. In the morning, as we prepared to board the coach for training, he noticed the blood on the forecourt. 'What the hell's gone off here?' Hall asked, probably knowing it must have involved me. The skipper, Paul Bowgett, pulled him to one side and said: 'There was some trouble last night. It wasn't his fault. He didn't cause it, but he ended up giving a couple of lads a terrible hiding.' The other players seemed to love it and made up their minds: 'You'll do for us.'

The Gateshead incident was remembered by Hall the day we played away against Stafford Rangers and I arrived at the station long after the train and the team had gone. I'd never been out of Hertfordshire on my own before, but knew I had to make it under my own steam. Somehow, thanks to a couple of other trains and a taxi, I got to the Stafford ground before the Wealdstone team. It had been well worth the sweat and the fares. Brian Hall made no bones about the importance of that journey. He'd just about had enough, what with my trouble with the police and the bloodshed at

Gateshead and he told me straight: 'You were finished if you hadn't turned up here. I would have cancelled your registration. You'd better sort yourself out.' It gave me the fright I needed.

I was nowhere near established in the Wealdstone side, but the team had made it to Wembley for the final of the FA Trophy against Boston. I was not chosen in the starting line up, or as a sub. They involved me, which was kind, but I couldn't properly enter the spirit of the occasion. I watched the game, in my tracksuit, from the Wembley benches. The boys duly completed the job to become the first team ever to win the Gola League/FA Trophy double.

* * *

With a new season coming, the driving ban was a pain. I needed to impress in training but to do that, I had to get there. One of my mates had a brainwave: 'Get yourself a little moped and a bleedin' great crash helmet so when you drive through the village, the local copper won't know you.' Wicked! That's exactly what I did. My Honda 90 (deposit paid by Mum as usual) was a kind of cross between a pedal-cycle and a motorbike – maximum speed 28–30 mph. Flat out. Downhill. With a following gale. It took me the best part of an hour to get from Bedmond to Wealdstone in all weathers, a parka jacket and the biggest, blackest crash helmet you've ever seen. What a 'trainspotter'.

My perseverance and determination to get to training, come what may, seemed to make an impression on Brian Hall. For instance, there were times when, as the other players arrived in their smart suits, I'd turn up in my building clobber – all mud stains and cement smears. If I'd been working in London, say, I'd catch a train and then a bus to Harrow and Wealdstone station and walk the rest of the way. Sometimes I'd get there an hour and a half early.

I was completely taken aback when Hally told me there were League clubs taking an interest in me. I wondered 'Is he just saying that?' because I knew he quite liked me for being a bit of a lad and that he saw I was as keen as they come.

It was around this time I came of age. At least, that's what's supposed to happen when you reach twenty-one, isn't it? Party time. What a stroke of luck that Mum and Dave had set themselves up as landlords at The One Bell in St Albans, the perfect venue for a party.

It would be the first time Mum and Dad and Dave and Jenny would all be together at the same time, so it was a bit tense to begin with. The party broke the ice but I can't say that ice was the only thing broken that night.

There were around a hundred invited partygoers, my mates from Bedmond, a few from St Albans and some of the lads from Wealdstone as well as the family. But it all ended a bit ahead of schedule when a group of blokes gatecrashed the party and started causing trouble. People were screaming, throwing punches, tussling all over the shop and tables were flying – the full monty. The police were called and order was restored, but the party was over. I remember thinking afterwards, though, that there was one important consolation from the night that ended in a complete shambles. I had my dad and stepdad fighting on the same side!

During the 1985–86 season I held down a midfield place in the
Wealdstone side and I was happy enough with my progress. In fact,
I still found it hard to believe I'd made it to Gola League level. But
then the lads started talking about a couple of players I didn't know,
until I went training one night and they were there, practising with
us, as if they'd never been away.

It turned out that during the summer months they had been
playing in Norway and Sweden. 'Hey,' I thought, 'there could be a
chance here. Sod the building game, this could be football full-
time.' They told me they went over in April and came back at the end
of November. They had had a terrific time. And guess who was the
bloke who arranged it all? It was only Dave 'Harry' Bassett, the one
who had us chipping balls over the hedge at Bedmond, now the
highly successful manager of Wimbledon.

I went to Brian Hall and asked him if there was any chance I
could be fixed up with one of those numbers abroad. Me! I didn't
really know where 'abroad' was! But I'd heard the banter: cash in
hand, flat provided, free food and a car and thought, 'This'll do me.'

Harry Bassett had heard of me. Derek French, Wimbledon's

physio, had lived in our village years earlier and taken me down there to train alongside the apprentices for a few days.

What I didn't know was that Wimbledon had sent Dave Kemp, now their assistant manager, to watch me playing for Wealdstone. So when Brian Hall contacted Bassett he knew a little about who I was. I went to see Bassett at his house and he said: 'I hear you'd like to go out to Sweden and I can arrange it for you. Providing you give me your word that there will be no fighting, no aggro, nothing.'

I couldn't get the words out quick enough: 'I really want this, I really want it badly. I won't mess it up, that's my promise.'

A couple of weeks later, with my first passport in my hand, I'm down to London and gone. I flew for the very first time. My skin-head days behind me, there I was with a mop of curly hair and some jeans and my boots in my old, familiar piece of luggage – the black bin-liner – out from Heathrow and into Stockholm. I knew I was in a foreign country when a geezer came up to me and said: 'Winee Djones? Winsent Peter Djones?'

He must have been thinking whatever the Swedish is for 'What the bleedin' hell do we have here?' as I walked off with him in my poxy sheepskin jacket, tracksuit bottoms (well-worn), old trainers and the black bag that was obviously almost empty.

'Winsent Peter Djones,' he said again. 'I am Burt Bustron, chairman of IFK Holmsund. We need, now, to catch the aeroplane.'

'What? I've just got off.'

'No, you do not understand. Now we must fly to the north of Sweden.'

It was a small plane heading for Umea, a tiny airport. Once on board he assured me: 'Yes, we are a very nice football club and we have big ambitions.' In fact, Holmsund were in the northern section of the Swedish Third Division. It turned out that I was about to play for the equivalent of Bedmond first team! Well, maybe a bit higher than that, but nowhere near Wealdstone standard.

I thought we were still above the clouds as the plane landed, because there was snow everywhere, four feet deep in most places. But that was only part of the shock because after we'd walked across the tarmac somebody opened a door and I saw the welcoming party: fifty or more media people waiting for us – reporters, interviewers, cameras of all kinds, lights, the works.

I was invited to sit down and had already started thinking: 'Don't let this be happening. This lot believe I'm something I'm not. Bassett has done a right sales job here.' He'd told me to say I was on Wimbledon's books but I didn't realise they were expecting a star. I told a string of porkies – I was in the Wimbledon side and, as a young player, had come to Sweden to get experience and keep myself sharp. All the time that press conference was in progress I was feeling guilty and regretting every minute of it. There it was, next morning, all over the papers – the long-awaited arrival of Vincent Peter Jones. And that's how they referred to me in print and on TV throughout my stay.

My regret about those little white lies was soon replaced by a sense of wonder as I was driven to my apartment. We went through a large town and beyond, up a road into the country for about twenty minutes. The scenery was stunning, with rivers and lakes, and there I was in the back seat thinking: 'This is bang on.'

And it all got better and better. There was another lad still to come out a few weeks later, Steve Parsons (of non-League pedigree with Wimbledon connections!), but I was to live with Mark McNeil, a centre forward with Orient. The apartment was beautiful – the ground floor of a typical, large Scandinavian house built of timber and overlooking the sea – three bedrooms, massive lounge, kitchen, a nice little garden. Oh, and a brand-new Saab saloon to share between the two of us. I thought I'd won the pools. 'We were told you like to go fishing,' the chairman announced. 'Well, we have a nice boat for you, with an engine.' The money didn't seem that important all of a sudden but it was still handy to learn I'd be paid £300 every fortnight, cash in hand.

Whatever sportswear I needed I was simply to choose at a huge store and charge it to the club's account: the full kit, boots, track-suits, even Astroturf boots. Choose them, try them on, admire yourself in the mirror and just sign for the lot. I knew, there and then, that I had to make football my life. Having had a quick taste of all this, the thought of returning to work on the building sites was terrifying. So was the thought of not doing well with Holmsund and having to be sent home ahead of schedule.

They don't mess about in Sweden. I was met at the airport, changed planes, did a press conference, checked in at the apart-ment, kitted myself out at the sports shop and made my debut all on that first day. 'We have our first pre-season game tonight,' they said, 'and we want you to play.' I could hardly refuse.

The venue was a bit like a leisure centre. A grey, gravelly all-weather pitch under floodlights, which looked pretty spectacular once they'd bulldozed the snow into piles eight feet high all round the place. It was a freezing night, but I wasn't prepared for the sight that greeted me when Mark led me into the changing-room to meet the lads. The players were part-time pros, most of them employed in 'dolly jobs' organised by the club. They turned out to be a terrific bunch of guys but they looked a right bloody picture to me, first off – all done up in tracksuit bottoms with long socks over the top, double shirts, gloves and thick bobble-hats. That was our strip for a pre-season fixture.

We won 6–0. There was no players' bar after the game, but we did get together, our boys and the opposing team, in the sauna. Cosy! It was a bit of a culture shock for me in the beginning: game over, into the sauna, then back home with Mark to cook a meal and watch a video. We normally played on Sundays so there was no going out on Saturday nights. The university disco was about the only place to have a drink, so I didn't bother – I gave it up. We did have barbecues at the players' homes on warmer evenings. That was the big night out for them and their wives and kids. The culture shock was a pleasant one and I welcomed the new routine despite finding it hard getting used to twenty-four hours of virtual daylight. No wonder the apartment had curtains as thick as duvets.

Twenty-four-hour daylight has its advantages if you're smart enough to adjust! I became friendly with a cod fisherman, Tom. Often I'd join him at 4am to help put out the nets. I made another pal who, if we didn't have a game, took me camping and fishing in the mountains. So I had the sea, the rivers, the mountains and the football. As close to perfection as I could get. The only thing missing was the shooting.

The game gave me a wonderful time as well. Mark and I turned into minor celebrities. The various divisions in Sweden have 'player of the week' awards and I won it more times than anybody. In fact, at the end of the season I was the winner of the Third Division trophy, nationwide, top choice from all of sections north, south, east and west. As Holmsund enjoyed the glory of being top of the table, I was lapping up the recognition.

The simplicity of our little ground just added to its appeal. It had

Holmsund. My time in Sweden persuaded me I had a career in football.

a smashing pitch and clubhouse, the obligatory sauna and some-where to have a cup of tea. Its capacity was about 2,500, mostly accommodated on wooden terraces. This was the venue for a mighty cup game against Djurgaarden, one of the country's major clubs from its top division. This was like, say, Manchester United playing Wealdstone away.

I asked Dad and Jenny out to Sweden for a week. My old man couldn't believe it, me signing autographs! He loved it in Sweden and even played in a specially arranged match between the players' fathers and the club coaches. Him and his skinny little legs, with my boots on scoring with a thirty-yarder. The bloke who'd been on Watford's books as a kid revelling in another moment of glory.

Djurgaarden's centre forward was Brian McDermott, the lad who used to play for Arsenal. As centre half, of course, I was the one who would mark him. The press had us both together for pictures the night before the game and I actually remember feeling starstruck.

They should have beaten us 10–0, especially after they took a 2–0 lead, but they reckoned without the centre half and the centre forward from the same apartment. I marked McDermott out of the game and my mate Mark McNeil just went bang ... bang ... bang ... wallop. He scored all our goals in a 4–2 win that seemed to confound the entire country. It was only the next day that we fully appreciated what we had done, when the national papers said we had pulled off one of the greatest giant-killing performances of all time in Swedish football.

Holmsund were finally knocked out of the cup in the semis, but by then Mark and I had returned to England. I had met three of the club's bigwigs sometime earlier to negotiate a new deal for the following season. They were offering me a £10,000 signing-on fee to be paid in instalments. If there had been such a thing as the lottery in those days then I'd have won it. That's the way it felt and I couldn't stop thinking about it while they took some time to sort out the details.

When I was next called in I was expecting to sign the contract on the spot. No hesitation. Especially when they said I could have the ten grand *and* £400 a week, tax paid. But I didn't sign. As soon as I stepped into the office they handed me a letter. It was from Bassett, handwritten, saying: 'Heard that you're doing brilliantly and that you're coming back next week. Link up with French on your return and come into Wimbledon for a month's trial.'

I returned to England with £1,200 I'd saved and one of the first things I did was buy my first 'posh' car – a Cortina estate – for £900. I rang Bassett within an hour of arriving home. I told him how well things had gone for me abroad and that I hadn't had a drink – a record I was to keep up for almost a year after returning.

'Get yourself settled,' Bassett told me. 'Give Frenchy a ring and come in on Monday.'

Wimbledon had just been promoted to what was then the First Division. I have to admit to being lucky with my start at the club because I was already mates with Wally Downes. Wally had been their first apprentice and was regarded as top man. He was a sort of combination of shop steward and piss-taker, and was regarded as Bassett's son. I'd got to know him at Wealdstone where he often came to parties and other dos. Straight away he put his arm around me, and no other initiation was required. The new boy was a mate of Wally's: I was accepted. I was in.

We had a practice match and finished with a cross-country run which you had to complete in under seventeen minutes. Right up the side of the A3, through the woods, up hill and down dale and back again and a lap round the public playing-fields, with Alan Gillette, the assistant manager, standing there, stopwatch in hand. Yes, as you might have guessed, I was at the front. I just bombed out there and left the rest behind.

On the way back, past the physio room above the caff, I could see all the heads at the window. Derek French opened it and yelled: 'Go on, our Jones boy!' It gave me a wonderful feeling, just to win that little race for Frenchy, the man who had urged Bassett to give me a chance. I knew he'd be, well, over the moon.

My first match was at centre half for the reserves at Orient and nothing special, then a night game at Feltham in strong wind and driving rain, which was bloody horrible. I was over-enthusiastic, wanting more than anything in my life to succeed, but not daring to hope too much.

There was an afternoon game during the third week of my trial, against Brentford reserves at the training ground, and for some reason they stuck me into midfield – probably because I hadn't been doing all that well at centre half. I took that as a bad sign. I thought I was down the road, out of there with the words all players dread: 'Well done, lad. We don't have an opening right now but we'll keep an eye on you.' In other words, don't ring us, we'll ring you.

And then I went and scored two goals in a 3–1 win. I just felt so comfortable in midfield, enjoying more freedom to run, winning all the headers. I learned, later, that Frenchy was urging Bassett to play me there. And something else happened during that match when Bassett and the others were sitting upstairs, watching through the office window. I took a throw-in. For no apparent reason I ran over the touchline, picked up the ball and launched it almost to the far side of the penalty area. I heard a kind of gasp and several of the players all letting out the same words at the same time: 'Fu … cking hell!' They'd never seen anything like it before and I didn't know I could do it either. Little did any of us know, then, that it was to become part of my trademark.

Alan Gillette came down one morning of that third week and announced: 'Jonah, Harry wants to see you.' The cry went up immediately from the other players: 'Go on, my son. Contract! Contract! Contract!' I went up those stairs not daring to even wish, just expecting him to say something like 'You're doing a bit better in midfield so we'll play you there a couple more times.'

Bassett came straight out with it: 'Jonah, you're doing well, son. Gonna take a chance with you. I'm gonna sign you.' It's hard to describe the feeling that came over me at that moment. I imagine it was a bit like dying, when everything goes, just seems to evaporate. I couldn't get a word out, never mind in. I stood there, stunned and gobsmacked, so grateful but completely bewildered all at the same time. I finally managed to gasp, 'Yeah, yeah, yeah.' And nodded my head repeatedly.

'We're going to give you the rest of this season and next season. Two seasons, then. And make sure you bloody well work hard.'

I'd heard about signing-on fees at Wealdstone and I'd been offered one to return to Sweden so I asked Bassett: 'Any chance of a signing-on fee or something?'

'No,' he snapped. 'I've given you your chance. You get in the first team and I'll look after you. Now fuck off.' End of contract negotiations. But Vinnie Jones was a full-time professional footballer with a club in the top division of the English game. Thanks again, Granddad.

Thursday was Bassett's day for picking the team. The only things going through my head were the thrills of training alongside professional players and having been rewarded with a contract a week before my trial period was up. I looked around me and saw lads who had been with Wimbledon for years but had never trained let alone played with the first team. For somebody who had been in and out of the Wealdstone side, well, it was enough for me just to be there.

The session finished with a game between the reds and blues. Those in the blue bibs would be the team for Saturday. That was Bassett's routine. Everybody stood and looked at one another when Steve Galliers, a stocky little midfield player, was told by the manager: 'Right, you swap with Jonah.' Other players stood and scratched their heads and, like me, were obviously wondering what the hell was going on as I was handed a blue bib and told to play in midfield. I didn't worry about Steve Galliers' feelings at that moment because I couldn't fully appreciate what was happening, the significance of it. I was just training.

But as we were about to start, the chitchat began. Wally came up to me and said: 'You're in.' In? Me in the Wimbledon side to play at Nottingham Forest two days later? I thought they should have put Wally in a straitjacket!

But it was true. Bassett named me in the side. It was like somebody saying: 'Right, you are now King of England. Get on with it.' I phoned my old man and my uncles who were all desperate to come to the game but I couldn't tell them, then, about tickets because I didn't know how to arrange them.

Bassett had lent me £150 to buy a suit. He insisted the players wore them on match days and I didn't have one. I dashed into London and bought a dark-blue suit and a nice white shirt to go with it, and treated myself to a new pair of football boots. And the first thing I did when I got home to John and Wendy's was put on my new gear with the official club tie and look at myself in the mirror.

I was rooming with Wally Downes in Nottingham. Wally had become my minder. He knew that I could handle myself and was a bit of a rebel. He'd also been told that I was a good pal to have. But I couldn't understand why he kept urging me to hurry up as we checked into the hotel in Nottingham. 'All right, all right,' I said, running to the lift. Once upstairs, Wally rushed me into our room and all I could hear along the corridor was laughing and the sound of running taps. The other players were filling their wastepaper-bins with water and those who were slow into their rooms copped it. Whoosh! It was what the lads called 'having a crack'.

That was only the start of it. Later two players found messages written in shaving foam on the mirror, bed-linen tied in knots, towels and clothes dumped in the bath with the water running. And there was no calling the chambermaid: you had to sort it out as best you could and get on with it. This was the law of the jungle with Wimbledon. The first time I'd seen it in action but I was to experience it hundreds of times more.

Wally told me quietly: 'That is why you guard your room key, our key, with your life.'

It was a happy and contented but extremely nervous twenty-one-year-old who eventually wandered off to his bed that night. I felt part of the scene as I settled down in my bed.

It was about 11.30pm. No chance of dropping off straight away because my mind was in a whirl, wondering what tomorrow was going to bring and remembering the specific instructions Bassett had given me about marking somebody called Neil Webb: 'Listen, son, this bloke could be the next captain of England. He's the dog's bollocks. Don't worry about playing football, just run around and stay with him and stop him playing.' The thoughts raced on until they were suddenly broken by the phone ringing. And it rang again and again and again, with various good luck messages: 'Lucky sod. First Division player, are we? Tosser. Shitting yourself yet?' They came from several rooms; even Bassett and Frenchy were kind enough to call.

Five minutes later – bang, bang, bang. I thought our door was about to be forced off its hinges. Wally jumped up, opened it and in they piled. Four of the players not involved in the match, and they had with them this old bird who, I learned later, was a legendary Nottingham Forest supporter nicknamed Amazing Grace.

I'm lying there, not able to believe my eyes and muttering: 'This can't be happening. Somebody please tell me this ain't happening.'

'Come on, Jonah,' they started. 'This is your initiation.'

'Piss off,' I told them. They were making a hell of a din and I could imagine Harry Bassett storming through the door at any moment.

'Go on, go on, Jonah,' Wally chipped in. He was rolling about on his bed, laughing like the rest of them.

I pulled the bedcovers up to my chin but there was no stopping the cabaret. The boys sat 'Amazing' at the end of the bed in front of the mirror and started helping her shed her gear. Off came her top, then her bra and I started shouting: 'No, no!'

I was close to panic but suddenly relieved when the lady in the looking glass announced: 'Let's have a drink. I've got to get a drink.' Surely that was the sign for them to get the hell out of there, but no chance. Two of the lads said they would go and get a couple of miniatures from the hotel machine.

The drinks duly arrived in style. Not a couple of miniatures but the entire bloody machine wheeled into the room! I was ready to quit, to leg it to another room, anybody's – anywhere but there. Wally could see the terror on my face. He wasn't just laughing any old laugh by this stage; the tears were rolling down his face.

Amazing rose to her feet and peeled off her remaining gear, stood in front of the mirror and then looked at me. 'If you come anywhere near me …' I said from my bed. She didn't. She turned, sat on the end of the bed completely starkers, facing the mirror. And then she started to sing.

'If you're happy and you know it and you really want to show it' she sang and stared at herself bouncing in the mirror and the lads were clapping and singing along as well. That's when something snapped. I'd reached the point where something just 'goes' with me. I was shaking as much with rage now as fear. I gathered up all her gear, thrust it at the lads and told the lot of them to get out of that room. They must have realised I meant it, because out they went.

I couldn't sleep, though. It was 1.30 in the morning, perhaps a little later, and I was still shaking. I'd imagined having a plate of pasta for dinner, a nice early night to prepare for my big day. And I ended up with a naked bird in the room and several choruses of 'If you're happy and you know it'. That was no way to prepare for a match, never mind your debut appearance, surely.

'But that's the chaps,' Wally said to me before we finally turned in. 'That's us. That's Wimbledon. We have players at this club like Dennis Wise, a free transfer. Lawrie Sanchez, twenty grand from Reading. We're not superstars, we are still lads off the street, playing in the First Division. And this is our spirit.'

From that day, or night, I knew the score and how I was expected to carry on. It was the first time I'd ever thought of that old saying: if you can't beat 'em, join 'em. Although, in the early hours of that particular morning, I'm glad I didn't!

The next day when we trotted out to warm up, I was hit by a weird sensation. The further I went up the tunnel the more I seemed to be shrinking, both physically and mentally. I was like Alice in Wonderland. When I actually stepped on to the grass I felt no more than twelve inches tall. As if I had gone from six foot to one foot in a matter of seconds. It was strange and it was scary.

Then the shakes started. I started to run, not to anywhere or anyone in particular, just running, headlong, round the sides of the pitch. Like Forrest Gump. The shakes don't show when you're running and I was hoping it would work the fear out of my system. Eventually I could feel myself coming together. I started to take in the scene around me, and then one of the boys pinged a ball in my direction. I pinged it back. It felt OK. For me, the whole mood and atmosphere changed the moment I pulled that first-team shirt, that No 4, over my head. It was a feeling I will never forget. The only time I matched it was at Wembley in the FA Cup final the following season. I tucked the shirt into my shorts and smoothed both hands repeatedly down my chest. God, did I feel proud. Everybody seemed to be willing me to succeed.

Our lads knew next to nothing about the Forest players. Wally Downes was up-to-date and knowledgeable about his football but eighty per cent of us in the squad didn't really have a clue. Funnily enough they didn't know any of us, either. We were the surprise packets who had suddenly made it to the top level, and that was our strength.

Intimidation was a big part of the ploy. Imagine Neil Webb's feelings when, with me standing alongside him, he had Wally yelling at him:

'You're going to get it today –

right in the mouth.' Webb spread his arms as much as to say: 'What's all this? I'm just here to play football.'

'You're going to get it anyway. First chance and we'll do you.' You turned round and John Kay would be saying the same thing to, maybe, Franz Carr. You'd be defending a corner and keeper Dave Beasant would be saying something similar to a couple of their players in the goalmouth. The looks on their faces said it all: 'What are this lot about? What is going on here?'

Not that it worked particularly well, that day. I was chasing Neil Webb everywhere and couldn't get near him. I kept thinking: 'I'm in the wrong place here, well out of my depth. This is not for me.' I honestly feared I was out of my league even though Carlton Fairweather put us in front after two minutes.

The rest of the Wimbledon side thought I was off my trolley twenty minutes later when, after Carr and Webb had swapped passes, the ball was swung high into our goalmouth. Beasant was stranded and I could sense Webb next to me at the far post. 'Don't let the bugger score. This is the one who's going to be the next England captain, mark him out of the game.' The thought rushed through my head. But instead of jumping and heading the ball, I was so determined he shouldn't get it – I punched it. On my league debut. Needless to say Nigel Clough put away the penalty.

And we were losing by half time after Andy Thorn deflected the ball into his own net. I don't think I touched the ball with my plastic-coated boots during those first forty-five minutes. I do remember going in for the interval and being thankful it was over. As we reached the mouth of the tunnel I tugged at Glyn Hodges' shirt and asked him: 'How am I doing?'

'Yeah, yeah, great. Just keep going.'

I wasn't convinced. Sid Neal, the kit man, who must have been in his seventies, came round with the tea in white plastic beakers. I'd never dream of having a cup of tea at half time these days, but I took one then. I was desperately in need of some reassurance as well so I asked Sid: 'How am I doing?'

A little hard of hearing, Sid tapped his earpiece and boomed: 'What? What you saying? How are you doing? Well, let me put it this way, you might as well give me that bleedin' shirt cos I could do a lot better than what you've just done!' I just thought that was that. The old stager could see I'd had a nightmare so that was me. Done. Finished. Back with Bedmond next week, probably.

The second half wasn't much of an improvement. Glyn Hodges' equaliser for us broke their rhythm for a while but Forest's Johnny Metgod made it 3–2. I was to start my First Division career in a losing team after all. End of debut. Thankfully, it was not to be the end of the world.

The only good thing that came out of the Forest game was that throw-in of mine, the long launch that I didn't know I had until I produced it, out of the blue, in training. Bassett seized on it the following week. He had me throwing it and throwing it and throwing it some more for up to an hour on the Thursday and Friday until I was putting it straight on to John Fashanu's head, or anybody else's who charged into the box. The week had started with me thinking I'd blown my big chance and it was probably because of that long throw that I was in the squad for the next game. It must have nagged at Bassett's mind. He had seen another way of getting the ball into the opponents' penalty area in one fell swoop, another way of setting up goals. He must have thought that if we practised it long enough the routine would begin to bear fruit. It was to produce 10–15 goals a season and at Plough Lane, our tight little home ground before the switch to Selhurst Park, I could throw the ball into the box from the halfway line. I think it saved my footballing career.

I must have had to get thirty tickets for my second game, my home debut. Everybody wants to see Manchester United anyway, and you can imagine the fascination among all those mates of mine … Vinnie playing against Alex Ferguson's mighty men from Old Trafford. Fascination? Disbelief, more like, until they actually clapped eyes on me coming out of the tunnel.

They were all there: Mum, Dad, the boys from Bedmond, everybody. Afterwards, it was as if that match changed something. It was different at the pub on Sundays. We all met for our usual drink but suddenly I was made to feel different, as if I had flown the nest and found myself at another level. Not higher or better than any of them because I always wanted to feel the same and still do, but different, certainly. I really tried to stay one of the crowd but events were going so fast and overtaking me. They had never been out of the Watford area, but I was to finish up going to the likes of The Hippodrome and Stringfellow's. But to this day I still manage to be Vinnie Jones, the pal who grew up with them, fought with them, drank with them, went out with them and worked with them. It was just that after I played against Manchester United, well, it underlined the fact that I had become a player.

I couldn't stop looking around me, that afternoon. I looked at the crowd and saw my friends and family. I looked at the opposition and had to keep reminding myself that all this really was happening at a time when I should have been just completing my month's trial. That I was part of a team about to play against the likes of Paul McGrath, Kevin Moran, Jesper Olsen, Remi Moses and Frank Stapleton. And Bryan Robson if he managed to get off the substitutes' bench. I was nervous but I was also keen to get started. No feeling small, this time, but with a sense that I had to say thanks in a way that was obvious to everybody. And with that need came a feeling almost of confidence.

I got my chance in the final minutes of the first half, when we won a corner on the right. We had players ready to attack at the near post, the far post and in the middle. I just stood there somewhere beyond the box until Brian Gayle said to me: 'You go first.' Me? Go first? This was my second game for Wimbledon, right? And I was facing players I'd only ever seen before in books or on the telly.

I started to make a run but then realised I'd gone miles too soon and would probably be alongside Glyn Hodges by the time he struck the corner! I stopped, began to walk back and realised Kevin Moran had gone with me. I was actually being marked by Kevin Moran, Manchester United's Irish international. So I ran again, really ran and as the ball flew in from the right I thought it was coming for my head. My head! In the box against Manchester United. I held Moran off with my left arm and threw my head at the ball. I didn't know where I was putting it, just thought, 'There's the goal, head towards the goal …'

Bosh! Perfect contact. Remi Moses still had his hand on the post as the ball sped for goal. He tried to head it and I thought he was going to knock it over the bar but the power of my header knocked him back. The ball hit the roof of the net and poor old Remi landed on his bum. I had scored against Manchester United!

I didn't know what to do, how to react. I just ran and shook an arm in the air and disappeared under the pile of team mates who leaped on me from all angles. It might seem strange, but at that moment I said another little prayer: 'Come on, Granddad, come on, please let it stay at 1–0.'

And he did. United did bring on 'Pop' Robson, but there was

nothing Captain Marvel could do to spoil my incredible day.

Afterwards, there was bedlam in the dressing-room. I had the next peg to John Fashanu and all the other players came over and took hold of me, yelling: 'Yeah, you've done it, Jonah. We've done Man United.'

Next thing, a steward put his head round the door and asked if I could go and talk to the press. The press boys rattled off their questions – and there were plenty of them because nobody had heard of me.

'What job did you do before turning pro?'

'I used to work with my old man on the buildings.'

'What sort of building work?'

'Well, digging out footings, hod carrying, things like that.'

It was out. The hod carrier was the label from that day. It was something I had to live with, the fact that the critics would seize it like vultures and shake it for all it was worth. When Jones became the target, up went the cry: 'Get him back on the hod where he belongs.'

I haven't liked that because, in their attempts to rubbish me, they have degraded many decent people. There is nothing wrong with carrying a hod for a living and I am proud to have retained the links with my background and my roots. Kevin Keegan, Bryan Robson, Alan Shearer, people like these were known only as footballers but I want people to say of me: 'He was nearly twenty-two before he became a pro footballer and he remains one of us.' I have tried to be their torch bearer in a way – working in a different world but knowing and appreciating where my world is.

I was on a roll. We played Chelsea away and won 4–0 and I scored again. Watford, the club who had turfed me out as a school-boy, came to Plough Lane and were beaten and I scored again. Sheffield Wednesday, seen off 3–0 at home and I scored again. I'd been in my first punch-up as well, although all my headlines were about the goals I'd scored rather than my bad behaviour in the beginning.

The trouble occurred at Chelsea but it was not of my making, I just joined in like everybody else. At Wimbledon, you see, everything was done with an attitude of 'all for one and one for all'. Doug Rougvie, Chelsea's big bruiser of a defender, a Scottish international to boot, went in on Dave Beasant and sparked off a free for all.

There was mayhem at Stamford Bridge with about twenty players involved in a right old bundle. Fash ended up on the floor, apparently head-butted by Rougvie and I ran in and went whack. Mine was not the only right-hander delivered into the general ruck. It seemed that everyone was in. We'd played only seventeen minutes and Rougvie was sent off for the incident with Fash. It was all over the papers, next day, and Bassett had us watch the video of the game in the office and warned us: 'It's good that we all stick together but we can't be doing this, lads. That was out of order.'

I sometimes think that Bassett took out my brain, reprogrammed it and put it back in. I was so grateful for the chance he gave me, so keen to justify his faith, so terrified that it would all be taken away overnight, so bloody determined to win every tackle, every ball, every advantage possible. And certainly every game. I became a different person when I stepped over the touchline. That weird shrinking sensation at the City Ground never returned. I was feeling bigger and bigger but was also conscious of this Jekyll and Hyde thing deep inside me. If I put my hand on my heart I have

What a start: John Fashanu, Dennis Wise and Andy Thorn help me to celebrate my goal against Manchester United on my home debut for Wimbledon.

to admit I have never been able to fully control it.

Once I started scoring, I couldn't stop. Or that's how it seemed until we played Charlton at our place. I was through on their goal-keeper, one on one. Another goal was a mere formality, but I put it wide. Another chance passed me by. Then I made a run that was timed to perfection, beat the offside trap and set myself up with another chance. Missed again. The goals dried up as quickly as they began with that wonderful moment against Manchester United. I didn't score another goal that first season.

But once I had stopped scoring I was made more aware of the other aspects of the game, the defensive rather than the attacking. That side of the game hadn't particularly concerned me before. All I was interested in was getting forward in support and hoping to get a goal.

The whole feeling at Wimbledon was so intense and frantic. It was hammered into us that we were playing for the very survival of the entire club. We felt under threat all the time – that if we were relegated then we would all be finished. Hardly surprising that trouble, big trouble, was just around the corner: Arsenal at Plough Lane. Graham Rix, former assistant manager at Chelsea, said some-thing to the effect that we shouldn't even be sharing the same pitch, never mind in the same league as Arsenal. I thought: 'Right, smart arse. You might be Graham Rix. You might be Arsenal. But now you're going to learn about Wimbledon and about me. You're going to find out who I am.' And I whacked him. At the first opportunity, I just lashed out. I was so caught up in the emotion of it all that I actually believed the other lads would think it was great. Not a bit. The referee came across and said: 'What do you think you're doing? There's no room for that on my pitch. Get off!' The reality of it all hit me like a sledgehammer. Get off. Early bath. I could see Bassett going berserk on the touchline and his anger was not aimed at the referee, either. I was in disgrace.

I walked off and headed for the dressing-room on my own. I've always thought that somebody should accompany a player sent off if only to show him he's still wanted, still 'one of us', instead of being isolated because of one mad second. But nobody walked with me and it seemed a hell of a long way. Once in the changing-room I just sat on my own. A dressing-room, in those circumstances, is the loneliest place in the world. I wished a hole would appear in the floor so I could jump right in. I would have given anything to slip back in time for the chance to ignore Rixy's wind-up, to be able to just run past him and get on with the game. I had let everybody down and I kept going over it, time and again, in my head: 'Why? Why did you let him get to you? Why did you do that? What the hell happened?'

People have asked me countless times and I used to ask myself what happens to me once I get out on that pitch. I'd see other players 'lose it' and I'd think to myself: 'What's he doing? He's a far better player than that – doesn't need to resort to that kind of stuff.' Yes, I asked myself the same question for ten to twelve years and still haven't found a proper answer.

I'm not really sure how the 'hard man' thing started but I began to get the feeling I was going to be the one the opposition looked at and chose not to mess with.

One thing I've never been able to stand is the thought of people looking down their noses at me. They do say you can take a man from the gutter but you can never take the gutter from a man. I think I've been rebelling against people with that attitude towards me throughout my football career. I adopted an attitude that said: 'I am off the building site and I'm representing ordinary working-class folk of this country. I know all about the Eric Cantonas of this world, with all their dosh. Great players but we're not all born like that. Some of us have had to work bloody hard to make it this far.'

Reminders of tougher days can be good for you. I peered from Frenchy's car one bitterly cold morning and noticed a group of builders. It took my mind back to desperate mornings when I arrived on the site wearing my balaclava. Everywhere frost-bound. The sand was so hard that we built a fire in an oil drum and stood it in a hole in the heap to start a thaw. As the sand gradually softened we could then begin to mix it and get on with the job – providing you could free your hand from the frost on the handle of the shovel.

It was like gazing at my own past: déjà vu. Those builders, with the oil drum in the sand heap, were doing exactly what we had done. They were in the real world, a world a darned sight harder than mine, but the building boys didn't moan. They worked their hands to the bone for £300-£400 a week but were as happy as any people I have ever seen, enjoying a few pints for a couple of hours on Friday nights.

Chapter 11

Harry was as much a part of the mischief-making as the players who were eventually to become known, nationwide, as the Crazy Gang. Tony Stenson, sports reporter with the Mirror and a Dons man through and through, came up with the nickname that described us perfectly and was then used by all the media. Stenson coined the phrase after a whole series of pranks, so-called initiations and general mayhem.

When we went to Portugal for a few days before an FA Cup tie against Portsmouth at Plough Lane, Bassett turned his back just long enough for Wally Downes and me to swipe his room key.

We came up with a beauty this time: whatever wasn't screwed down in Harry's room, we removed. The bed, dressing-table, television set, chairs, lamps, the lot. All to be neatly assembled elsewhere. And everybody was there for the climax as the lift doors opened and Bassett stepped out – to find his room laid out before him, in the lobby. It was set out exactly as it had been originally. Bed, here, dressing-table, there, telly to one side, towels neatly folded and all his belongings just as he had left them. His match notes were there as well, detailing players with specific tasks at set pieces, but the notes had slight adjustments: the kit man and Pat from the caff were substituted for Bassett's original choices.

A few days later, before the Portsmouth game, he really wound us up, telling us we were going to get beaten and constantly calling us 'poofs'. We were so keyed up and ready to go. On the Friday, Fash and I daubed our faces with the whitewash used for marking out the pitch. It was our warpaint, although, as I said at the time, it showed up far better on Fash than on me!

We slaughtered Portsmouth to such an extent that their manager, Alan Ball, said he was ashamed of his own team. We were on BBC's *Match of the Day*, for once, and I was having an absolute blinder, winning the tackles and the headers and feeling absolutely inspired. I wanted to be in on everything, part of every move. Not long into the second half I caught Mick Tait with my arm in a pretty hefty challenge and was booked, but otherwise I was doing really well, until, with less than half an hour to go, Bassett pulled me off and sent on the sub. I must have been man of the match but it made no difference. I was blazing, my eyes were standing out of my head. I must have looked as if I was on cocaine or something.

I went stomping round the dressing-room yelling: 'Why's he done that? How could he bring me off? Why, why, why?' Alan Cork was in there and came to put an arm round me but there was no calming me down. I charged across the room and head-butted the wall. Bang, bang, bang! I actually put a dent in the surface. Corky just said: 'Bloody hell' and ran out. Apparently he went straight to Frenchy and told him I was nutting the wall, wrecking the dressing-room. Even when the game finished and the others came in I was still at boiling point. My fists were clenched and I was yelling: 'Where's Bassett? Bring him in here. Just let me get hold of him.'

Frenchy realised what I intended doing. And this time, there was no quiet, fatherly advice. He went absolutely mad at me. He dragged me into the showers and said: 'Now you bloody well listen to me. He's the manager. He's the one who gave you your big chance in the game. He makes the decisions and you can't do this to him.' I had never seen Frenchy freak out before and the shock of it calmed me down immediately. He made sure he acknowledged that I had played very well, but also made it crystal clear that if I whacked Bassett I'd be throwing everything away. And what happened when Harry walked in? Typical of the man: 'Hey, Jonah,

Jonah,' he yelled across the dressing-room. 'Brilliant today, son. You had a real go at them. Brilliant.'

It was like putting a pin in a balloon. He just flattened me. If that dressing-room had been quiet enough I swear we'd have heard the hiss of the anger escaping from my ears. My arms relaxed, my fists uncurled. What else was there to say but, 'Thanks, boss.'

That match was one of the first times I'd ever been in action on TV so I couldn't wait to watch the highlights that night. The commentator (I'm sure it was John Motson) suddenly announced: '… and there's going to be a substitution. Yes, it's Vinnie Jones and that's a sensible move by Bassett because if he hadn't been brought off he could well have been sent off.' That was when the message got home. I'd been substituted for my own good and for the benefit of the side.

*   *   *

Dave Bassett has been a kind of God in my life. I admire him more than anyone I've ever worked with and he will tell you, even now, that if ever I have a problem, I dial his number. He remains an important father figure to me. He created me, gave me the chance and encouraged me to make the very most of it.

Wimbledon had survived in the First Division, which was a fantastic achievement for a little club that had been elected from non-League into the Fourth Division only ten years earlier. Bassett's priority was to make sure they stayed up in that historic first season at the top. But it was not to be, not with Bassett, anyway. One morning during the summer break, it was all over the back pages: Bassett goes to Watford. I thought it was the end of me and the end of my world. Nobody but Bassett would put me in their team. He knew how I felt about his managerial style, he knew I was a Watford boy, but he hadn't asked me if I fancied going with him and I couldn't understand why.

In fact, he was to invite me a couple of months later, asking me down to watch the game and have a chat. I went eagerly. I think they played Swindon that night and afterwards Bassett took me into the boardroom and said: 'I'd like you to meet Elton John.' If only the boys could have seen me, shaking hands with Elton John!

'So you're a Watford boy,' Elton said. I told him how my granddad had been a supporter at Vicarage Road and we nattered on about Wimbledon's successful first season at top level and, of course, about Harry Bassett. I was at ease with Elton because I could see he was so in love with Watford and that he liked Bassett's reputation and attitude as an all-out winner. It was the start of another era at Watford, just as it was to be at Wimbledon, and I sensed they would quite like me to be part of it.

'Right,' Harry said. 'I'll have to go through the proper channels and have a word about buying you.' As I was about to leave, Elton asked, 'Vinnie, what are you doing now?' I came out with the sort of thing you are not supposed to say to the chairman of a football club about to try and buy you: 'I'm going up the pub.' And immediately thought,

'Mistake, Jonah. Clanger.

Shouldn't have said that.'

'Which pub?'

'The Bell. I drink at The Bell in Bedmond.'

'How far is it? How long to get there?' I couldn't believe this was happening. Elton John, world megastar, asking me how long it would take to get to my local boozer. Somebody wake me up.

'About fifteen to twenty minutes,' I said, still believing he was only making polite conversation.

'All right if I come with you?' Was he being serious? It was only a fleeting thought. Nah, this must be one of Bassett's wind-ups, with Elton more than happy to be part of it.

With no more ado he arranged for his driver to come round and pick him up in the Roller and follow me up there. A few of the boys were in there as usual but I didn't say anything the second I walked in because I wanted to wait until Elton had had time to park up. But as he walked into the bar I announced: 'Meet my new mate, lads!' There were more open mouths than in a mass audition for Oliver! Nobody said anything for a few seconds but Elton broke the ice, began the football chat as if he had been a regular among us for years. He was just one of the chaps. Brilliant. Within ten minutes the pub was jam-packed. He stayed for about three-quarters of an hour until the usual problem: everybody and their aunt wanting autographs. He obliged umpteen times before coming across to me and saying: 'I think I'll shoot off. Thanks a lot.' It was only after he had gone that we discovered he had left £50 behind the bar. Drinks for the boys – what a star!

The proposed move to Watford didn't meet with Wimbledon's agreement and, as things turned out, it would probably have been the wrong time for me to go there. Bassett got the sack, Elton sold the club and I didn't see him again for many years until we met at the Brit Awards.

* * *

Bassett's departure from Wimbledon gave me a chance to jump in. It was the first time I really got to know the club's owner, Sam Hammam. I fancied my chances of a new contract, so I went straight to the top, to Sam's offices in London's Curzon Street. He upped my wages from £150 a week to £350, and this time there was a signing-on fee of £7,000 a year.

But when a new manager arrives at a club you just don't know what the future holds. Our new man for 1987–88 turned out to be Bobby Gould, who had called at a few places both as a player and manager. It was not an easy situation for him. We were all Harry's boys and none of us thought there could be much of a life after Bassett. Wally Downes was among the first to get the axe, and it was soon obvious that one or two more would be on their way.

Gould made an immediate impact by signing Keith Curle from Reading, for £500,000. Half a million quid for a defender. That was unheard of for Wimbledon. Not only that but Gould made it clear right from the start that he would do things his way, and had no room for anybody who wanted to live in the past.

The new arrivals came thick and fast: John Scales, Terry Phelan, Clive Goodyear, then Eric Young. And somebody else, somebody who caused a lot of eyebrows to be raised not only at Plough Lane but also throughout the country: England coach Don Howe. Wimbledon had adopted a kind of 'them and us' mentality and Howe was certainly regarded as coming from them. Nobody thought for a moment he would want anything to do with us. It was Gould's attempt to change the club, to alter its controversial image and introduce an air of respectability and professionalism.

Howe's arrival had us thinking, 'There is going to be life after Bassett, after all.' He was sensible but he was fun, as well. He enjoyed the banter, the crack, and that surprised us. He came to me one morning at training and said: 'I think we'll have one of those army songs. Come on, Vinnie – up to the front and start it off.' So there I was, leading the jogging, chanting the way the American troops do with the other lads echoing the words, sentence after sentence. They felt like prats at first but Don got them at it: 'Come on, lads, all in it together.'

Don tried to teach us that you can respect your opponents without offering the initiative to them. You can have fun without being irresponsible. There is a line that should not be crossed. His and Gould's hardest task was making sure we stayed on the right side of it.

Personally, I was feeling a bit more grown up and responsible, anyway – not that many would have noticed! I left Johnny Moore's place shortly before Bassett left Wimbledon. I bought my first ever house – a three-bedroomed semi in St Agnell's Lane, Hemel Hempstead. It was a joint venture with my mate Steve Robinson who split the £48,000 asking price with me on a joint mortgage and, before long, Kerry Coles – Colesy's dad – moved in as well. He'd been on his own for years and we were glad to have him. At least he kept a bit of order in the house.

As opposed to trouble in the camp.

There was plenty of that, a couple of months into the new season, when I did my first newspaper interview that involved a fee. We were due to play Liverpool at our place on the Saturday and Steve Howard from the Sun linked up with me. The deal was that I would be paid £250 for the piece.

I'd talked to journalists before. The casual, quick chat after matches but nothing on this kind of scale. I didn't even have thirty games under my belt by then so I was a bit green. It was all going nicely, nothing particularly controversial, how was I approaching the Liverpool game and what it had been like to play against them at Anfield the previous season. But then came the question that taught me a lesson about dealing with the press. Steve suddenly hit me with something that had happened at Anfield, something that I thought was known about only by me and Kenny Dalglish.

'What's this I heard about you telling him you'd rip his head off?'

I was staggered. I thought: 'Where the hell's he heard that?'

Being naive, I trotted out the details.

Dalglish had been playing up front for them at Anfield and when I went in to tackle him he caught me a treat – studs first, right on the shin. It really shocked me. I just looked up and said: 'What's your game?'

Then the verbals. 'Oh, shut it.' Dalglish said and began belittling Wimbledon. The man was supposed to be a legend. I couldn't believe what I was hearing. He was the one who had caught me with a late tackle, not the other way round.

So I told Dalglish: 'Oh yeah? Well if I get near you once I'm going to rip your head off and crap in the hole.' I had to come back with something and it was the first thing that entered my head. It was something I'd heard in a film, a smart reply in the heat of the moment, and I thought no more about it.

Steve phoned me later on and warned there could be bother in the morning. He told me the reporters had no control over the way stories were displayed. The 'ripping off the ear' remark was being picked out in large letters. Of course it was. It had been toned down a little, having me threatening to remove the ear rather than the head and spitting in the hole, but it was still the story. I'd know that now, but I hadn't a clue then. I hardly slept a wink that night; I was almost in tears and my stomach was turning over and over.

By the time I arrived for training, next day, there was bedlam. Journalists and cameras everywhere. I was called in to see Bobby Gould and he went ballistic. I'd been getting along quite nicely and then, wallop! I'd dropped my guard and got caught with a beauty. Once Gouldy had calmed down a bit and mentioned leaving me out of the side that weekend, he tried to warn me about the press, about taking great care in what I said.

I have had some right run-ins with Steve over the years and he still giggles about that one. He's got skin thicker than an elephant's. Although I hadn't appreciated or expected the impact my own words would have, I was made to feel guilty about what I had done. And by the end of the month, I'd faced my first charge of 'bringing the game into disrepute' and been fined £250. So the interview brought no reward at all – only a bloody nightmare and a load of old hassle.

There was a young lad up on Tyneside who was making a lot of headlines and exciting all the good judges of the game. At twenty, Paul Gascoigne was on the brink of the full England side – commonly regarded not only as an outstanding midfield player but also as potentially one of the greatest footballers this country had ever produced. I had missed our League game against Newcastle at St James' Park. We'd won 2–1, but Gascoigne had completely torn Wimbledon apart. Something clearly had to be done about him for the match at Plough Lane.

'This boy Gascoigne is something special,' Don Howe told me. 'For this one game we want you to forget about your usual role in the team and simply mark this player. I know you are capable of doing that job and it has to be done or, otherwise, we lose the game. Just think about it carefully, get it into your head that you simply have to mark the one man.'

I had pretty much sorted it out in my mind by the Saturday afternoon when I pulled up at the ground and saw a hell of a lot more cameras than usual outside. Gazza was coming! And Mirandinha, their Brazilian import. So there was going to be a bigger crowd than average at Plough Lane and those were the players the people had come to see. As I ran down the tunnel all of a sudden something went ping in my head. Bobby Gould had said to me in training: 'Just get yourself in his way. The art of being a good player is to do it genteelly.' That was it. I thought to myself: 'I'm going to do him – genteelly!'

From the first whistle I was there.

I eyeballed Gazza and he eyeballed back. He started making silly runs to wind me up but I didn't need any winding – I was pumped up anyway: teeth gritted, veins standing out in my neck. We hadn't been playing more than five minutes when he turned and asked, sheepishly: 'Are you all right, mate?'

'I'm all right, pal. But you'd better get used to this cos there's another eighty-five minutes of it coming your way.'

'We'll see about that.' Gazza grinned. But every time he got the ball I was on him. Every time they tried to pass to him I jumped in front. Every time he tried to run past me he was shoving, using his body. Quite physical, but I could tell I was doing OK, I was preventing him from doing his stuff. There were a few verbals, as there usually are in the course of the game, although more has been made of it over the years whenever I was involved. I told Gazza he was 'bloody fat' and he told me I was 'bloody thick'. The only time I was allowed to leave Gascoigne's side was to take my throw-ins. But I had my doubts at the very first one. Even when I was signalled to go and take the throw I shouted across to Gazza: 'Fat boy! Wait there. I'll be back in a minute.'

Other players heard it and there were a few chuckles but I don't think Gascoigne could believe his eyes and ears. I noticed him glance across to the Newcastle bench with a bemused expression on his face as much as to say: 'Where's this geezer coming from? Fruit and nut, him.' The longer the game went on, the more deflated he became. Instead of trying to get away, he began marking me, standing close up at set pieces. It was then that I remembered what John Cornell, my first-ever manager, told me as a kid. Remember? 'If an opponent is marking you a bit tight, reach behind you and give him a little squeeze. He won't get that close to you next time.'

My chance came with a free kick to us. I was facing the ball, he was right behind me, so close that he whispered: 'Hey, shouldn't you be marking me?' Just reach behind you … I moved my left arm backwards and grabbed his knackers. As he tried to pull away, startled and shocked, I held on and gave a little squeeze. Genteelly, of course. Gazza didn't squeal. Well, not a lot. I think he tried but no sound came out. He got on with the game after we 'parted' and I'm certain that, like me, he thought no more about our little get together. The game ended as a goalless draw and although there might have been a gesture or two out of place I felt happy that I'd done my job. Happier than Gazza at half time, apparently, because I was told later that he'd gone in shaking and in tears. He must have been frustrated.

I was heading for the bath when somebody shouted, 'Jonah, Jonah,' and a steward came through clutching a red rose: 'Mr Gascoigne would like you to accept this.' Excellent! Where the hell he'd found the rose I had no idea, but it was a fine gesture worthy of response. I immediately looked round for something to send in return. I spotted the toilet brush on its stand so I grabbed it and said: 'Take that back for him with my compliments.'

It was an amusing end to a bloody good day and there were no hard feelings between Gazza and me. We have had a laugh about it since. It had been a spur-of-the-moment thing, not done with malice. What I didn't know was that the photographers had captured the moment. Something that happened in seconds was frozen for all time – and plastered all over the back pages. The headlines staggered me. 'Psycho!' 'Nasty!' 'Crazy Vinnie!' 'X-Certificate!' 'The Ugly Face of Soccer'. Was it really that serious?

I was already developing a reputation as something of a tough guy and I didn't like it. But after that incident, which looks far more severe in a still shot than it was at the time, people started to say:

'This bloke's a complete hoodlum.'

It wasn't so much that I was being portrayed as a hard man but more as some kind of monster who was out of control. Not really a footballer, and anyway, he came off a building site so what do you expect? That kind of attitude. What killed me was that I'd done such a good job in marking a skilful player out of the game for the benefit of my own team. I didn't regret doing it because I knew I had pleased Gouldy and Don Howe and that they appreciated the contribution I'd made from the footballing point of view.

The notorious photo of me grabbing Gazza – a trick I learnt when I was a young lad playing against older boys.

It was only because it was Gazza that the response, elsewhere, was so hostile. How could somebody like me dare to stop a talent such as his? There I was, being congratulated and slapped on the back in the dressing-room yet about to be hammered in the newspapers. The subject was brought up for months.

Bobby Gould tried to put it all into perspective when he told the press after the game: 'I asked Vinnie to look after Gascoigne and he did. He did one hell of a job for the team, so let's not be making him out to be the villain.' He did take me to task for what he regarded as unnecessary risks and provocation. But he was equally keen to applaud and encourage the aspects of my football he regarded as valuable qualities within the side.

It was never my football that would make me famous; it was that picture with Gazza. I was carrying a stigma, I suppose.

It wasn't all bad news, though. Something else had been ticking along for Wimbledon. A nice run of results from matches that featured the familiar cry from Fash: 'Put it in the mixer!' as keeper Dave Beasant prepared to clear the ball by aiming to drop it deep in the opposition's half. In the mixer and everybody in after it, the hairs on your neck standing up with the excitement and your opponents thinking, 'We don't need this. Let's get it over and done with and out of here.'

The mixer was stirring up a Cup run. It couldn't be that Wimbledon, scruffy, hard-up little, under-talented, over-physical Wimbledon, with that hod carrier who grabs people by the crutch, could be on their way to Wembley. Could it?

* * *

Most of the publicity seemed to centre on Big Ron Atkinson prior to the start of our FA Cup adventure. The flamboyant, popular manager of West Brom was bringing his side to our place, but most experts preferred to wonder whether it was going to be Big Ron's year for the trophy. Nobody gave a second thought to Wimbledon's chances. So we were expecting a tough old game against Albion but didn't get it. We trounced them 4–1.

That victory gave us a good feeling. We deserved it and there was a fresh mood of optimism in the dressing-room as the whole place vibrated to the rock 'n' roll of Little Richard. There was a lot of yelling and singing and somebody, I think it was John Fashanu, began the chant:

'The Dons are on the march again.'

I didn't have any gut feeling about the Cup then, but I started to wonder after we beat Mansfield, away, in the fourth round. Maybe it was the fact that our defender, Terry Phelan, scored his only goal of the year, or maybe it was Dave Beasant's penalty save that secured our 2–1 victory, but something certainly set me thinking.

Where next? Where else but Newcastle. St James' Park for a massive Cup tie exactly two weeks after that match at Plough Lane. By now I felt the 'old Wimbledon' had joined forces with the new regime, that something special was beginning to develop. Yes, I began to have a feeling that all things were possible.

Unfortunately, I discovered it was impossible to make my peace with Newcastle before the Cup game. I had planned to fly up to Tyneside and have a photograph done: Gazza and me, all smiles and no ill feeling. But the idea was killed off by Newcastle's manager, Willie McFaul. Apparently he wanted none of it and somebody said he had threatened his players with fines if they joined in pre-match publicity.

Ah well, get up to Tyneside and get the job done. Most people believed it was the end of Wimbledon in the Cup, anyway. Those Geordie fans can certainly make themselves heard, especially when there are almost 30,000 of them up for the Cup. Their passion for that old silver pot is fiercer than anywhere else in the country.

We were inspired by the atmosphere of the place. Final whistle, 3–1 to us and, bloody hell, we're in the quarter finals.

Watford next. My old club, the one that rejected me but still my club at heart. They'd already beaten us twice in the League but when you are on a roll negative thoughts don't enter your mind. This was the Cup so this would be different. If you can win at Newcastle you can sort out Watford at home – and we did, 2–1, to reach the semis.

Against Luton at White Hart Lane, we were 1–0 down and on the back foot until we got a penalty. Fash placed it, a couple of steps and dinked it, calm as you like. Nothing cool about our reaction, though. We were screaming at one another: 'Come on, we can make Wembley! The bloody FA Cup final! Come on!' I noticed the look on the Luton players' faces. It was a look that said: 'This lot are going to

go on and win.' And we did, with a goal from Dennis Wise that kind of cannoned in off him as he went in for a tackle. I've never even bothered asking whether he meant it.

There is no sensation to compare with how you feel when the referee blows the final whistle that confirms you're going to Wembley. And I know there's nothing worse than the whistle that tells you you're not – as happened to me and Wimbledon in 1997. I just threw my shirt into the crowd at White Hart Lane the rest is a blur of total happiness. The nobodies had made it and proved that if you want it enough, love it enough, work at it and believe in it enough you really can get there.

On our way to victory over Luton in the 1988 FA Cup semi-finals.

The one or two of us who thought the week leading up to the final against Liverpool was going to be nice and easy couldn't have been more wrong. The squad was told we were going to prepare properly for this and we were made to train as hard as at any time all season.

We were given a hell of a boost with word from the Liverpool camp after their last game. Garry Gillespie and Nigel Spackman had gone up for a ball and cracked their heads together. They needed stitches and it became the talk of the Wimbledon boys all week. 'They're not going to want to head it at Wembley. They're not going to fancy too much of Fash. There's no way they will be one hundred per cent.' Even wearing fancy headbands!

The preparation was a credit to Don Howe and his complete knowledge of the game. Wisey would be employed on the right instead of the left side of the field and held deeper to counteract the threat of John Barnes. Although we frowned and wondered at first there was such a tone of confidence in Don's voice that real belief began to develop and to spread.

Each player was told what was expected of him. In my case it was straightforward: I had to win the battle with Steve McMahon.

The thought of defeat never entered our heads. We planned things down to the last detail and I clearly remember watching goalkeeper Dave Beasant thumbing through his little book on the game's penalty takers and which side they tended to hit the ball. Nothing was left to chance.

On the eve of the match it was off to the Cannizaro House, the swish hotel on Wimbledon Common. Out on the patio Bobby Gould announced he had a little gift for all of us. His mum had knitted us each a doll: Wimbledon colours, all blue and yellow and wearing black football boots. We all collapsed when it came to the No 9. She had knitted Fash's doll in black. Brilliant!

Fash, my regular room mate, and I were setting out for a walk after dinner when we were confronted at the bottom of the stairs by a bloke we sensed was a press man even before he spoke.

'What are you up to, mate?' I asked.

'I'd like a word with Fash,' he said. 'We've had a tip-off that you're messing around with this woman.'

This woman, as he put it, had apparently done some story with the News of the World for the Sunday after the final. 'Don't know what you're talking about,' Fash told him. And I said, 'You'd better get your arse out of here' before we called our agent, Eric Hall, and Gouldy to sort it out. Fash and I went back upstairs.

I was trying to unlock the door to our room, a really solid door, probably oak, when all of a sudden Fash's expression changed. It was the first time I'd ever seen John Fashanu lose his cool. He let loose a proper right-hander. It left dent marks in the surface of the door and the impact drove his knuckles into his hand. It came up like a balloon and he thought he'd bust it. Panic! I phoned down for the physio, Steve Allen, who was sure there was no break but the damaged hand had to be bandaged, and we had to report to the manager downstairs.

'Listen,' Gould told us, 'this is going to be the biggest day of your lives. Nothing must distract you. Forget the rubbish that's just gone on, it's all part of life and you'll have to deal with these kind of things from time to time. Let's just concentrate on what we're here for.'

Gouldy was about to move off but then stopped, turned to Fash and said: 'Right, here's a few quid, get all the boys together for a few jars down the road.'

It was a good move because rumours had swept through the hotel and the players were concerned and beginning to wonder what had gone off. It was about eight o'clock and we all joined ranks and walked to The Dog and Fox in Wimbledon.

The crack soon started in the pub and the worry turned to laughter again. 'Hope she's a welldy!' somebody shouted to Fash – a playful wish that 'this woman', whoever she was or if she existed, had been a Page 3 type, well-endowed. 'If she's ugly, Fash, your street cred will be down the drain.' He took it in that lovely way of his when he knows the crack's on him. He's serious and dry but a little smirk appears on his face and he gives a little nod of approval.

As it turned out, there was a front-page piece on the Sunday, some allegation of an affair, but it was thankfully nothing that caused too much upheaval for Fash and it soon blew over. Back at the hotel, Gouldy greeted us at the door: 'Everything all right, lads?'

'Yeah, boss, everything's fine, couldn't be better.' You could see the relief on his face. We were back on track and it was typical Wimbledon. Us against the rest. We were bonded, anyway, but that night glued us together.

I lay in bed that night, unable to drop off, my mind racing. All those friends and relatives were going to be there. My nan was going to the first game of her life, all my uncles – Dad's five brothers – dressed up in yellow and blue top-hat and tails, Mum with her new husband and Dad with his new wife. And I was flying Ann, besotted by her interest in horses, home from Italy where she had been working at a riding stables and returned speaking fluent Italian. And all the boys from Bedmond and the rest of Hertfordshire where I had so many friends. More than a hundred people of mine, in all – Christ, I hoped I wouldn't let them down.

I needed a word with Granddad. I didn't ask him for a winner's medal. There were three things going through my mind. 'Please don't let me be the one to make a crucial mistake. Please don't let Steve McMahon do me. And if there's any chance of me scoring, Granddad ...' I didn't get complete assurance from him. It's not like that when I talk to Granddad, there is nothing guaranteed. But I did drift off to sleep with the feeling that we were all going to be all right.

I was awake and out of bed at 6.30am. Well, a player shouldn't miss a moment of FA Cup final day. Fash was still sound asleep and

I knew there was no waking him. It always cracked me up, looking across at his bed, blankets pulled right up and the only thing showing was this little brown nose. He loved his sleep and always kept the curtains drawn tight until we were leaving to catch the coach. If ever I did wake him he'd go barmy and tell me to get out of the room.

The moment I woke that morning, the palms of my hands began to sweat. They were to stay like that throughout the entire day and the following day as well. However much I tried, I couldn't keep them dry.

Once washed and shaved, I gave Dennis Wise a ring.

Wisey, like me, was hyperactive. We needed something to do – anything to occupy us for a while, we were so excited. I said to him: 'I want to get my hair cut. I'm going to have the old short back and sides.' Before I became a professional player I always thought footballers should have a haircut and look smart on match days.

'Right,' Wisey giggled, 'lovely. That's what we'll do, then.'

We were full of beans, even before breakfast, and Bobby Gould must have read the warning signs. 'Now, you two have got to drop down a gear. You must calm down or you're going to be burned out before the match even starts.'

As soon as Gouldy turned his back, Wisey and I dropped the shoulder. We were out of there, into the car and cruising through Wimbledon High Street. It was still early, but we noticed a lady walking alone wearing a Wimbledon scarf. We slowed alongside her, wound down the window and yelled: 'Way-hey, go on you Dons!'

Bloody hell, it was June Whitfield, then of *Terry and June* fame. I didn't know it at the time but she was president of the Wimbledon supporters' club. She wandered over. 'All right, boys?' We chatted for a while, and she smiled her nice smile and said: 'Good luck to you and the team. I'll be there this afternoon.'

And we shot off, found a little Italian barber's and steamed in. The bloke was startled, saying: 'You're early, lads. First ones of the day.' Then he looked gobsmacked as he said: 'You're not …?'

'Yeah, just a quick trim for the pair of us,' I said.

'You're not …?' he repeated at least twice and I think he actually pinched himself. On a sudden impulse I asked him if he could do something different. He cut my hair down to a point at the nape of

the neck and then shaved up both sides to meet the longer stuff –
almost like a Mohican. My old man never let me live it down.

Back at the hotel, the preliminaries had started. You could sense
the atmosphere, the feeling of excitement and anticipation as soon
as you walked in. It was electric – the directors and club officials,
families, relatives, all sorts of people were out on the patio, every
one of them wearing a smile as if to say they were going to enjoy
every single second of the day, win, lose or draw.

On the coach, the customary card school got under way and we
kept glancing at the television screen showing Liverpool leaving
their hotel, and Wisey shouted: 'Look at them – they don't fancy it,
lads!' He was right. They looked as if they were on their way to a
funeral.

Our spirits were probably too high, if that's possible. Gouldy
walked up and down as we filed off the coach, frantically trying to
calm us down as if to say: 'Keep the lid on it, lads. Keep some of it
bottled up until you get out there.' Something did stop us in our
tracks a bit. We were all a little bit miffed at being given the away
dressing-room. But only until we walked into the place – all tiled, a
little bar in the corner with a geezer standing behind the Lucozade
and the bottles of water. On the left was what looked like a small
swimming pool – a massive bath, really deep – and a little further
on, the showers and the medical room. I stood and looked around
the place and thought: 'This is out of this world. This is Wembley.'

We strolled out to the pitch ahead of Liverpool and it was a
terrific feeling – no sense of pressure apart from the still-sweaty
palms. Fash and I strolled together, and I spotted my Uncle Colin in
his top-hat and tails, and then my mum and the rest of the family.

Wembley wasn't full at that stage but it was eighty per cent red.
There was one small pocket of blue and yellow, singing and waving
banners 'Vinnie Bites Your Legs' and 'Corky's Got No Hair – We
Don't Care'.

I can remember, vividly, back in the dressing-room, taking off
my suit and shirt and hanging it on the peg and thinking: 'The next
time I put this lot on I'll have played in the 1988 FA Cup final.' The
butterflies felt more like eagles and they were right up to the back
of my throat.

The buzzer sounded, time to go. As I stepped into that tunnel
I felt twice my normal size. My arms and legs felt massive. I knew

I could run for a week, never mind an hour and a half. We all knew our preparation had been perfect and that we had peaked at exactly the right time. The Liverpool players were in the tunnel first. They had come out quietly but we came out roaring. Literally roaring. The Liverpool boys looked completely shocked and the stewards stepped back out of our way.

Spackman and Gillespie were wearing ridiculous headbands and they took some terrible stick: 'Look at them, they daren't head it this afternoon. No chance. This is our day, boys.' The more it went on the more pumped up we became and it was as if we were actually growing physically on that slow march to the halfway line while Liverpool shrank further and further into their shells.

There is nothing to match the sensation that hits you when you walk from the mouth of that tunnel. The first sight is like a horseshoe made up of tens of thousands of faces amid dazzling colour. All those faces, for some reason they all seemed to be white faces standing out, peering among the flags. I looked around and it was a mass of red and white like a wall from the Royal Box right round to

Battling it out with Steve McMahon in the 1988 FA Cup final.

the other. Bloody hell! But then the blue and yellow Wimbledon support brought together like never before, bless their hearts. 'Not bad, this,' I thought. 'Not bad at all.'

For twenty minutes after the whistle went we worked our socks off, didn't let them win the midfield, shut them down, didn't let them play the way they wanted. Don Howe's words were going over and over in my mind and then Steve McMahon had the ball. As he shaped to receive it, I started running at him knowing exactly what I was going to do.

I took a chance that he would let the ball come across him and open out with it on the inside of his foot. If he'd just stopped that ball I would probably have been sent off. If he'd just touched it backwards, I'd have buried him. I gambled on meeting him head on with a proper solid tackle on the ball. It turned out just like reading a book. As I arrived he opened up, lovely, and my momentum took me in – wallop! I met the ball and saw his legs go up in the air. I was on the ground looking up at him as he was coming down on his back.

Some pro, Steve McMahon. Even on the way down, he was thinking, and as he landed he caught me with his elbow underneath my left eye. It split and bled and the mark still shows sometimes. My lifelong reminder of a close encounter on the sacred turf.

As I leaped to my feet all our players were shouting: 'Come on, Jonah, get in there.' I had won that tackle but, for some reason, conceded a free kick! But the point had been made, because that incident threw Liverpool off their game. After that, they had one eye on the ball and the other on our players every time we went in for a tackle.

Suddenly there was bedlam.

A free to us from wide of the box and I stood on the edge in case the ball wasn't cleared. Alan Cork made his run, Lawrie Sanchez stood his ground and got in a header. I saw Bruce Grobbelaar transfixed. It was as if he had just been set in stone. There was nothing he could do but look behind him and down. I looked down to where he was looking and the ball was behind him in the net and the roar battered the eardrums. We had scored! Wimbledon had scored at Wembley. There had never been any talk of us scoring and we were as shocked as anybody in the crowd. But what a wonderful, fantastic, unforgettable feeling it was.

Half time brought panic stations because we were sure the only thing that could beat us would be ourselves running out of steam. Don appeared and told us: 'Get your shirts off and wrap yourselves in these.' He had filled the bath with cold water and soaked a load of towels. Big towels, bloody freezing, but we duly obliged. It was to cool the blood on a steaming hot day but it would have taken more than wet towels to properly reduce the temperature of the Wimbledon team.

Especially when referee Brian Hill gave Liverpool that penalty in the second half. We knew Dave Beasant had done his homework on John Aldridge's penalty kicks. I stood there praying that Aldridge would take his normal bloody pen. He hit it the way our keeper thought he would and Dave Beasant made history with the dive that brought the first ever penalty save in an FA Cup final.

Everything became frantic.

Liverpool sent on Craig Johnston, the Aussie, a right busy bugger and the last person you need against you in those circumstances. Then Jan Molby came on and had a shot that whipped just over our crossbar. We were hanging on, Cunningham came on for Corky to do his little bits and pieces and keep the ball, then John Scales was off the bench as well. I called to him because he was standing in front of me: 'Scalesy! What are you doing? Where are you playing?' He hung his hands by his sides, frowned and said: 'Don't know. He said something like, "Just roar about up front."' But time was running out, and we held on to our 1–0 lead.

The final whistle in a Cup final you have won is the most beautiful single sound imaginable. Fash and I were ecstatic. We all were. Andy Thorn jumped on Beasant's back, Gouldy came running on and leaped into my arms and Don was still being Don 'Mr Cool'. The injured lads and those who hadn't played at all joined us.

We clapped the Liverpool team as they went up for their losers' medals and Gouldy warned us: 'Now you be gentlemen and do the right things.' Up went Beasant, with Wisey behind him, and the rest of us followed. You grab a hat, a scarf, and shake as many hands as possible up those steps. A medal from Princess Di and a kiss from Sam Hammam and, with no disrespect to either, you wished it had been the other way round!

Back on the side of the pitch I thought about all the stick I had

The Crazy Gang line up with the trophy.

taken over the time leading up to that day. I wanted to locate the press and give them a wave. One of the players shouted: 'Bassett's in the gantry.' He was doing some TV work and I grabbed the Cup and held it up, and as Harry looked down I became all emotional. I filled up but I screamed at him: 'For you, Harry. This is for you, son. This is yours.' And I pretended to throw it up to him. The very bloke who gave me the chance I had prayed for.

There were people everywhere

at Plough Lane. The place was seething and somewhere along the ten-yard walk from the coach to the entrance I was hit by what amounted to a rugby tackle. It was my old man, as happy as I'd ever seen him but crying his eyes out all the same. He spun me round and they were all there – Mum, my nan, my sister and God knows how many more relatives and friends. Looking round I saw the other lads surrounded by their families as well. Everybody wept tears of joy – it was like one of those scenes from the old newsreels of troops being welcomed home from war.

We seemed to be swept along on a tide, into the huge marquee where we all had our own table of ten. We hadn't been in there long when a steward tugged me and said: 'Percy's at the gate.' Percy had been a big Wimbledon fan for years. He used to come to every game, a real passionate supporter who would shout 'Give it to 'em, Vinnie' and glow and beam when I spotted him in the crowd and shouted back: 'All right, Perce.'

'He's with his missus,' the steward said, 'and reckons you told him that if Wimbledon won the Cup he could have your tie.' So out I went and Percy was in tears as well, as emotional as the rest. He has a handicapped child who he takes to games and looks after, and maybe twice a year he'd phone and I'd get him into the players' lounge. Yes, I'd struck a deal with him so it was off with my tie and I said: 'Here you are, son.' I draped it round his missus's shoulders and I knew I had to do something more. 'Come on, son,' I told him and had the gates opened so they could step through and come and join me among all those at my table for the meal and the entire evening of celebration.

It was good to have Ann there to share it all. My sister had lived with Mum in Watford while she finished her schooling, and after doing a couple of jobs went off with a school pal to be a stable-girl

in Bologna. We didn't have a lot to do with one another but we never lost touch, and I had to have her there for the final and all that followed.

The crowning glory, as all Wembley winners enjoy, was the bus tour on the Sunday. The mayor, the town hall balcony, the thousands of people lining the route and gathered in the centre. Fabulous memories of an event that could never be repeated – certainly not for a lad who once paused while mowing the grass and prayed for just one chance to be a professional footballer.

There was only one way to end a perfect weekend. Down at The Bell with all the Bedmond boys on Sunday night. It was the start of more celebrations that went on and on and on, for the best part of a week!

Chapter 14

To Coventry by Ferry

By contrast, I couldn't have had a worse start to Wimbledon's 1988–89 season as Cup holders, well, pre-season, to be accurate, playing a friendly on the Isle of Wight. I don't know whether it was for the benefit of one of Gouldy's mates or just a favour or how it came about, but we found ourselves playing a village team in Shanklin at what seemed to be the annual fete.

You don't expect to land in it during a friendly on the Isle of Wight, but it happened. After a corner, some geezer gave Dennis Wise a smack. In I went without hesitating and there was a right old bundle. Me and one of their players, Dave Woodhouse, went down, arms and legs flailing. I jumped up and looked round and expected the referee to come over and say something to us, but he stormed over and waved the red card. Get off! Just me! And then there followed another load of publicity about the use of the elbow.

I realised Bobby Gould was becoming brassed off with me. He had tried to tame me and couldn't and he'd had enough because I was affecting the credibility, the name of the club. And he was quite right. These things keep cropping up – I get myself involved, then hate myself afterwards. Travelling home on the ferry, I was sent to

Coventry. Nobody was allowed to talk to me, although Wisey took a chance and had a word or two. Gouldy gave me a right dressing-down when we got back, not the normal, friendly heart-to-heart, but a clear warning that he'd had enough and wasn't prepared to defend much more of it, if any. To be honest, our days looked numbered then – even though I was to see out another season at the club.

The newspapers made a great issue of the incident, of course, and I believe that the less you say, the quicker it dies. But Gouldy was doing interviews saying he'd stuck up for me enough and announced: 'I'm banning Jones from the club, indefinitely.' To have said that I think he must have given Sam Hammam an ultimatum: him or me. Whatever, it meant I didn't know whether I was going to play for the club again or whether they were going to sell me. I only wanted to play for Wimbledon. I dreaded the thought of leaving.

The suspension lasted for quite a while but, like most things, time healed the rift. I didn't make the side for the opening game of the season but we lost heavily and I thought: 'Right, Gouldy, now you're going to need me.' I was soon back in. And everything was going well enough until we played at Tottenham, and I got involved in an incident with Spurs' England international Gary Stevens.

I was somewhere around the centre of the pitch when Fash, shielding the ball by the touchline, had Stevens alongside him try-ing to nick possession. They seemed to be jockeying for ages so I started running over. I was almost there when Stevens did get the ball but he was still half tangled up with Fash. I went in with a block tackle on the ball and went right through with it sending the two of them flying. Throw-in to Tottenham, no free kick. Both players were down on the floor receiving treatment. Fashanu got up but Stevens didn't. He tried to play on, eventually, but his knee was all over the place and they took him off.

There was no way that I went to 'do' Gary Stevens. As I was run-ning over towards the pair of them I was sure I was going to make it and get the ball. I went in strong as I usually do, and the linesman was so close he was lucky he didn't become part of the tackle as well. There was a lot of hooting and hollering, the referee spoke with his linesman but it remained a throw-in, not a free kick. I still had to make a smuggled exit from White Hart Lane. There must have been about 500 Spurs fans gathered outside like a picket-line. Don Howe brought his car round to one side and I got in the back and crouched on the floor. Don spread his coat over me and was able to drive away unhindered and take me home.

I still believe Stevens was the victim of one of those things that happen in football. There doesn't always have to be a malicious reason for serious injuries. I think he had experienced quite a bit of knee trouble before and that one block tackle had been too much.

Some argued it was reckless, that there was no need for it. Everybody is entitled to an opinion, but if I'd gone in recklessly there would have been as much chance of my injuring Fashanu as Stevens – and it's hardly likely I would put my best mate at risk, is it?

The next morning I called at a newsagents, bought a whole bundle of magazines and headed for the hospital, hoping to see Gary. The lady on the desk picked up the phone: 'Mr Stevens, there's a Mr Jones here to see you.' A little pause and then she told me he didn't want to see me.

'Have you told him it's Vinnie Jones?'

'Yes, he knows. And he doesn't want to see you. He won't let you go up.'

I thought he'd still got the hump, which was fair enough, but I hoped that in the cold light of day, when he saw the video of the incident, he'd know there was nothing intentional. So I left the magazines and asked the receptionist to make sure he got them. They were just sports magazines I'd picked up at random – all sorts – football, boxing, golf, fishing, I'd scooped almost every kind from the shelves.

I picked up the paper the next morning to find a big piece about Gary Stevens' career being over and look what a sick individual Vinnie Jones is. That I'd visited the hospital and brought boxing magazines to a bloke about to go in for an operation! There was no mention of the other mags, all the other sports, just boxing. The press gave totally the wrong impression and I believe Gary still blames me for what happened. I wish, 100 per cent, that my tackle hadn't resulted in ending his career, but I don't suppose anything I could say would change his mind.

What happened at Goodison Park in February 1989 was something else. It wasn't the sending-off that annoyed me; it was what occurred after I tackled Graeme Sharp that still makes my blood boil.

Sharp was a tough lad, a Scottish international striker with a reputation for not allowing anybody to take liberties. My challenge was a stretching tackle – I was reaching too far, not trying to hurt him. Never in a million years. But I caught him late and on the top of his foot and he went over. Other players involved themselves and as I jumped to my feet Everton's Kevin Ratcliffe came charging over and confronted me, close up. So I stuck my chest out and put my head forward and, in the heat of the moment, said: 'Come on then, if you want it, you can have it.' I didn't thrust my head at him. I swear I was inches away and never made any contact.

But he flew backwards, hit the deck

and clutched his face as though I had nutted him. If he did that nowadays, video evidence would put him in deep trouble and in disgrace. I might be many things and have made many mistakes but nobody could ever accuse me of play acting or feigning injury to land a fellow pro in trouble.

I had already been cautioned for a foul on Peter Reid, so I could accept the dismissal for one yellow card after that because the poor tackle on Graeme Sharp deserved another. Two cautions and off, no argument. But there was no time for the referee to book me for the Sharp incident before Ratcliffe had dived in and keeled over. So I was sent packing for something I didn't do.

Don Howe went absolutely ballistic – with John Fashanu, who had led the protests on the pitch, but particularly with me. 'What am I doing here with you thugs? You're barbarians. This is me finished at this club.' I just sat there and didn't dare open my mouth. I always thought the world of Don Howe. There was no benefit of the doubt for me. I protested my innocence in the Ratcliffe incident, but the headlines condemned me all the same.

Sam Hammam was the one person who stood by me through everything. To this day, Sam will tell you I didn't touch Kevin Ratcliffe. He believed me, because whenever I did wrong I admitted it to him. I was always honest with him. I went to see Sam at the end of the 1988–89 season because I was becoming a mental wreck with all the publicity. Nothing was ever mentioned about a single pass or how well I might have played. I'd been on chat shows, Wogan and Jonathan Ross, and it was the same story: 'Why are you the hard man of football?' And then, at the end of the interview, a red card. Things like that were beyond a joke.

Sam and I talked for hours. I was trying to persuade him to sell me: 'I have to wake up to the newspapers every day. I have to walk into the training ground and face the lads. We get a great result but it's always the negative stuff in print and I'm beginning to think that even the other players have had enough of it. Maybe, Sam, Wimbledon Football Club without Vinnie Jones could start to gain a bit of credibility.' Sam was already in tears and by this time so was I. But he handed me my coat and said he'd think about it. And as I walked out of the door he added: 'Vin, things like this … people I love … I make very quick decisions.'

Four or five minutes away my new car phone rang. It was Bill Fotherby, managing director of Leeds United.

'Vinnie, I've just had Sam on the phone,' he said. 'We can meet with you today and he wants the deal done. If it's going to be done he wants it doing today. And no agents. Sam doesn't want any agents involved and if it gets to the press the deal is off.'

I was told to drive to the Oxford Street offices of Top Man, their sponsors, there and then. Sam Hammam, true to form, had made his decision very quickly. I was on my way to Leeds United.

As soon as I walked into those Oxford Street offices I saw Bill Fotherby, director Peter Ridsdale – now the Leeds chairman – and Alan Roberts, a kind of marketing man at the club, all waiting with a bottle of champagne standing on the table. There were handshakes all round and then the first question.

'How much a week would you want?' Ridsdale asked.

I was on £500 a week at Wimbledon and I didn't really know what figure to go for so, thinking in a hurry, I just trebled it then thought that was a bit much so I knocked off a hundred quid and said: 'I'd want £1,400 a week.'

'Yes, all right,' Ridsdale said

without batting an eyelid.

'And I want twenty-five grand a year signing-on fee. And a car.'

The words had hardly tumbled off my lips when Bill Fotherby stood up, leaned across the polished wood table, spat on his palm and said: 'Done. Here's my hand, it's a deal.' And we shook on it. Peter Ridsdale, who I was to discover to be a really sincere, lovely fella, opened the champagne. I was a Leeds United player, just like that, subject to the no-problem medical examination the following day.

I should have asked for a fifty-grand promotion bonus!

It was hardly surprising that I quickly developed a good feeling about Leeds and their people. The thing that immediately struck me was that everybody connected with the club was crackers about it, even the tea ladies. A bit different from one of the groundsmen at Wimbledon who used to tend to our pitch and then shoot off to watch Queens Park Rangers.

What I couldn't take was the resentment from the group of players who feared their days were numbered. Quite a few new signings had been made, including Gordon Strachan, Chris Fairclough, Mel Sterland and Mickey Thomas. Youngsters like David Batty, Gary Speed and Simon Grayson were on the brink of breaking into the side. But there were others, like Ian Baird, Bobby Davison, Mark Aizlewood, John Sheridan and Brendan Ormsby, who didn't seem sure about where they stood and they'd formed a bit of a clique. A big changeover in personnel was taking place and I had arrived in the middle of a situation where there were clearly two camps.

One day I'd had enough of all the whispering and sniggering. I just leaped to my feet and confronted Davison.

'No, no,' he said, 'you've got the wrong end of the stick.' Like hell I had. That lousy atmosphere had been simmering, building up over a period. I smacked him in the mouth and announced to the other twenty-five or thirty lads in the room: 'This all stops, right here and now. If any of you want to say anything or do anything, here I am.'

I stormed out and marched off to the changing-room to collect my gear and leave. Gordon Strachan had come out behind me: 'You all right, big man? Come on, calm down.'

'Fuck them, Gord. It's us and them. I've not been brought up with this kind of situation. I'm used to everyone being together. I can't handle this, I want out of this place.'

'Hey, hey, hey, big man.'

The voice of Mick Hennigan, one of the coaches, boomed from the corridor. 'The gaffer wants to see you.'

I thought I'd done it again and was right in it with my new boss for whacking one of the players and confronting all the others. I walked up there thinking I'd go back to Wimbledon.

Howard Wilkinson is one of the coolest men I've ever met – so confident, so sure of himself and with that uncanny ability to convince others they should believe in him as well. In that blunt Yorkshire accent of his he said: 'Sit down, son.' I sat there thinking I was ready to deal with anything he could come up with. I was steaming about what had just happened. 'You've disappointed me a bit, son. I've just been down to the players' lounge. Can't find one speck of blood in there.'

And then he told me the story of how Leeds came to pay £650,000 for me. He had sat in the stand at Highbury with Mick Hennigan at one of the last games of the 1988–89 season, when Gouldy had brought in an overseas player, Detzi Kruszynski. He was the kind of player who only wanted to perform when he had the ball; he wasn't interested in defending, picking up the runners. I was screaming at him to do his job, to go with his runner, but he let another one by and Arsenal almost scored. There was a bit of a bust-up and the referee had to separate us. Wilkinson had been there to watch Arsenal but he'd turned to Mick and said: 'That's the man we want.' He'd seen leadership qualities in me he felt were vital to sorting out his dressing-room and establishing the collective spirit that would give Leeds their best chance of promotion from the old Second Division.

From that moment in the manager's office, the problem was sorted and I was far happier. Confronted by the clique at Elland Road, I had found myself desperately missing the togetherness at Wimbledon. I had everything and the training was fantastic, I'd never been fitter in my life, I completely trusted Wilkinson and what he did and the belief in him from his other players was total. And yet I would return to my hotel suite feeling so depressed and lonely that I often sat on the end of my bed and cried.

I missed John Fashanu really badly and he was upset that Wimbledon had been prepared to let me go. I'd lost my big brother and in those weeks of trouble at Leeds, ninety-nine per cent of my phone calls were to Fash. He started to come up and see me on Wednesdays, our day off, and it was his support that got me through those worrying early weeks.

Howard Wilkinson's reaction to the dust-up that sorted out the Leeds boys gave me fresh confidence as well. I felt wanted and needed and gradually we started to become a close-knit force. It

was like the early Wimbledon days with Wally Downes, Glyn Hodges, Mark Morris and the boys, but without the crazy antics. We were very disciplined and proper at Leeds – you wouldn't go in and turn over Gordon Strachan's hotel room! Dave Batty became my best mate. Like I did as a kid, I used to go to his house for tea even when he wasn't in because he lived with his mum and dad. His dad was a dustman and his mum a supermarket worker and they were both very down to earth, smashing people. I suppose it was the family involvement that I wanted. They made me feel so welcome.

Everybody was wondering whether Gordon Strachan or I would be captain for the new season. I thought I might have a shout, seeing that the gaffer had signed me for leadership, but it was a masterstroke by Wilkinson when he made Gordon Strachan skipper. He was a great player in his own right, had the respect of all the others and he became a great captain. I was to be idolised at Leeds and could do no wrong, but there was no doubt that the wee man with the red hair was the right choice.

The 1989–90 season was a massive one for Leeds; they were desperate to get out of the old Second Division and back among the big boys. The Elland Road fans loved me and the feeling was mutual. That much was proved after I'd left the club and then returned to play against them for the first time. I was given a standing ovation from the entire crowd. When I came off, the groundsman, John Reynolds, told me: 'Only two ex-Leeds players have ever come back to a reception like that – the great John Charles and now you.'

To this day I get the same reaction whenever I go back. Leeds were a big part of my life and career. They were a club who had been living in the past, still glorying in the achievements of the Don Revie era, but Wilkinson bravely blew all that out of the water. He took down many of the old pictures because he was determined to build a new, modern Leeds United and turn it into a fortress again, proud of itself, not dwelling on the successful years that had long passed.

People have always argued that I was most effective playing for teams who were fighting for their lives. I have admitted to this Jekyll and Hyde thing within me, that I do change once I cross that white line five minutes before kick-off. I am two different animals. But with Wimbledon I actually played my most constructive football when they were comfortable in the table, not scrapping to avoid

I really enjoyed my time at Leeds and David Batty became my best mate.

relegation. I was far more composed then.

But it was all so different at Leeds. I knew what Gordon Strachan meant when he told me to concentrate on passing the ball more, but I didn't realise how much of an opportunity I would have to do exactly that. I played the best football of my life with Leeds because I was able to perform with a smile on my face. In fifty-three appearances I was booked only twice – against Swindon at home in September 1989 and at Wolverhampton the following March, both cautions for minor fouls. And I scored five goals.

It was different, you see. There was not the same kind of tension, week-in, week-out, no threat of relegation. Every time we went out – and I had the same feeling at times when I was at Chelsea – I was thinking: 'We're going to win this game, no problem.' There was a confidence in our ability, a self-assurance, a sort of aura about the team that I never experienced at Wimbledon, who had so often been the underdogs. The belief and trust in Howard Wilkinson, his preparations and attention to detail had us head and shoulders above other teams.

The club had a bit of a dodgy spell late in the season after going about ten points clear. Our luck had run out as well and Sheffield United were catching us. We needed to win at Bournemouth in the last match to clinch the championship, a beautiful sunny day with thousands upon thousands of Leeds fans down there – about 2,000 able to get into the ground and what seemed like another 10,000 outside. Chris Kamara did a bit of magic down the right, crossed and Lee Chapman scored. Leeds were champions and poor old Bournemouth were relegated.

For me the feeling was the nearest I'll ever get to the elation of winning that Cup final against Liverpool. Coming home was brilliant. At a supermarket on the way back, the manager gave Mel Sterland and me fifty quid for a few crates of beer and we all had a good drink along the way. With Howard Wilkinson, as usual, sitting at the front of the coach drinking his Glenmorangie and smoking his big Havana, just as he did on the way home every week – win, lose or draw. Everything he did, even the clothes he wore, had class.

Fantastic memories. A great manager, great lads, great results and great fun. At Leeds, we were all laughing by the end of that season and everything in the garden was rosy. Or so I thought.

Our victory against Bournemouth on the last day of the 1989–90 season clinched promotion to the top division.

Leeds had been desperate to get out of the old Second Division so we were ready to party...

Chapter 16

Giving It Both Barrels

On my return to Leeds for the start of the 1990–91 season, I found the name of Gary McAllister by my peg in the dressing-room. My heart sank. I'd come back in such high spirits, so confident, and Wilkinson hadn't breathed a word to even hint that I might be surplus to requirements.

The uneasy feeling that greeted me made no difference to my attitude in training, however. I still worked and worked. It must have been pretty impressive because Colin Murphy, manager of Lincoln at the time, came to watch us on one occasion when we were doing 400-metre stints on the track. Afterwards he told me if he hadn't witnessed somebody training like that, he'd never have believed it. He later wrote me a lovely letter saying: 'You have something special – never lose it or become disheartened.' I still cherish that letter.

When the first line-up was announced, Wilkinson didn't even have me among the substitutes. That really broke my heart. Somebody wandered up to me and said: 'After all you have done for this club, I can't believe you're not even sub.' I filled up. I had to leave quickly because I would have broken down. I couldn't understand what was going on but it didn't take a genius to work out that my days at Leeds were numbered. Around the fifth game of the season, away to Luton, I still hoped that I would be back in the side. I'd been doing some shooting up in Leeds and was planning to take my kit on the coach because I was due to stay the weekend at the old man's. Everybody was on the coach before me and, as Wilkinson went to get on board, I said something sarcastic like: 'Will I be needing my boots today?' He was not amused. When I opened the boot of my car, an idea struck me.

I took my shotgun from its sleeve and as the players looked out from the coach I saw their expressions change and everybody went deadly silent. As I stepped inside Howard looked up and I put the barrels of the twelve-bore right up his nose with my finger on the trigger and said: 'Now are you going to bloody play me at Luton?'

I kept a straight face long enough for him to seriously wonder. Of course the gun wasn't loaded, and the safety mechanism was in place but, for a second or two, he looked a bit worried. And then, as I replaced a scowl with a smile and then a laugh, Howard cracked up. He was the first to appreciate the gag and the laughter went through the entire coach even though the lads were saying: 'How dare you pull a stunt like that on the gaffer?' But that's me and Howard knew, and he appreciated it more than anybody. And the real laugh was that he played me at Luton, though again he had the final word by pulling me off.

I trained like a Trojan again on the Monday, with even more of a spring in my step, only to be taken aside by Wilkinson later, and told: 'I don't know whether you're interested or not but I've had Dave Bassett on the phone. I don't want you to go. I want you to stay here but it's up to you. You've been great for this club and I'll support you in whatever you decide.' I was speechless. It was like somebody telling the Queen she was on her way out of Buckingham Palace. I had been at my happiest with Leeds, playing proper football and loving the whole professional feel about the place. Now this.

That evening, I met Sheffield United's assistant manager, Geoff Taylor, who took me to Bassett's house. I had already made up my mind. It doesn't matter what you have done for a club, how you feel about them and about leaving, you are very much on your own in those circumstances.

My dad, however, was really against the move. 'Sleep on it, sleep on it,' he said. 'Do you realise where Sheffield United are? They're at the bottom of the First Division.'

But I signed. They were paying me a grand more a week than Leeds and Bassett wanted me in as captain, but in footballing terms I was going backwards. Overall, my season at Bramall Lane was a fairly depressing experience. We were losing a lot of games and I was being made man of the match on a pretty regular basis just for having a go. I was back to the brawn and the aggression and the bookings were flying again right, left and centre. There were spells where the players didn't dare even go into town because of the bad reaction from the fans.

Bassett was getting increasingly worried. He had brought me in as a leader and eventually asked me what I thought we could do, because if we didn't do something, we'd be going down, as we were bottom of the table at the end of January. We talked for a while and he made his decision: 'Go and tell the boys that I'll put a hundred grand in the players' pool if we stay up.' It was all above board – how much you received depended on how many games you played – and maybe it was coincidence that we went on to win seven match-es on the trot, which took us up to twelfth, and so we survived.

Not that I was completely miserable all the time at Sheffield. I rented a cottage close to a golf course. I had split up with my girl-friend, Mylene Elliston, at Wimbledon, and although I had started seeing her again after the Cup final we had grown apart in my time at Leeds. She had a very good job as PA to the governor of a London bank and so we saw less and less of each other. But after the move to Sheffield, I started going back to Watford more, linked up with Mylene again and she joined me at the cottage. There was one particularly good night out we had and the eventual result of it was broken to me in a casino at Luton.

'I've something to tell you.'

I half expected what was coming next. 'I'm pregnant.'

I didn't go all gooey and silly. I just went 'Phew.' I was well pleased.

During her pregnancy, everybody was telling me: 'This is what you needed. This will settle you down. This is the best thing for you.' Not in my case. Some blokes do change their personalities and characters, but I still go with the flow.

That close-season we had been to the house Mylene kept in St Albans, loaded everything into the car, including the dog, and were on our way back to Sheffield when she began to suffer what I thought must be stomach cramps. 'I'll be all right,' she said, so we kept driving up the M1. After all, there were six weeks to go before the baby was due. Somewhere around Leicester Forest East her waters broke. I didn't know what that was all about but on phoning Jessop's Hospital in Sheffield I was put into a right panic because they said: 'Bring her straight here.'

The baby was on its way. I was really frightened for Mylene because of all the pain she was obviously going through. The doctor was saying, 'No, it won't come,' and all I could see was a small space and what looked like a big head.

'It's never going to come out,' I said, all of a sudden the expert gynaecologist.

'We'll have to use forceps.'

I couldn't believe my eyes – they were massive things. But suddenly the baby was out: a boy. Covered in blood and as the nurse passed him to me they hadn't separated the cord. I was just motionless. They smacked his bum, put a tube in his mouth and then I was able to hold him for a minute. I didn't say a word. I was completely speechless but I felt ten feet tall. Until the doctor told me to hand him back to Mylene and my legs began to shake, out of control.

'Come on, then,' I heard the doctor's posh voice say to me. 'Come on, let's go and wet the baby's head while these people tidy things up.' I gave Mylene a kiss and I kissed him – the baby, not the doctor. Within two or three minutes of the birth I found myself in the pub right next to the hospital.

'Another one?' the landlord said to the doctor.

'Yes, yes.'

He had a pint of beer and I had a pint of Guinness. There were one or two locals in, a couple of them saying: 'You the father, then? Congratulations.' It was the doc's routine to go in there following births during opening hours. All the locals knew him and knew the score – brilliant! I don't remember much, only that I wanted to ask him about babies and he wanted to talk to me about football.

We called our baby Aaron. His arrival thrilled me to bits. I went out with a couple of the players and got drunk out of my head. I was so proud, I don't think there was a person left in Sheffield who hadn't heard. I rang the world!

Mylene was always very independent. I had first met her at Batchwood Hall nightclub in St Albans where she worked to earn extra money to pay her mortgage. We were both overjoyed at Aaron's arrival but I hadn't expected the difficulties we would face. Our situation began to change, which wasn't Mylene's fault or, of course, the baby's, but rather the overall circumstances. A mother under pressure, a baby crying and a professional footballer worried about the lack of sleep. I found myself tiptoeing around her, trying not to trigger off a mood.

Eventually, Mylene started going back to St Albans more. Then she stopped coming up to see me and, in an attempt to sort out the future, I suggested we bought a house and moved in together. Her place was her security, her worldly goods, so that suggestion didn't work. Instead, we reached the stage where I was driving down from Sheffield to St Albans to see her and Aaron.

But drastic change was not far away. While I was at Mylene's on a day off the phone rang.

'It's Dave Bassett for you,' said Mylene.

'All right, Harry? What's going on then?'

'Jonah, how are you? Listen, I've agreed a fee with Chelsea for you.'

I have to say the prospect of getting away from the crash-bang game I'd returned to and joining the likes of Dennis Wise at Stamford Bridge came as a huge relief. I drove to the Posthouse at Heathrow and signed for Chelsea within an hour. Another fee of £575,000 and another 'double your money' contract.

Within weeks, I joined my furniture at 5 Hunters Oak – a new house I'd bought at Wimbledon at the place they nicknamed The Footballers' Estate – seeing Mylene only when I went round to see Aaron. Joe Allon, the centre forward Chelsea had signed from Hartlepool, and Kerry Coles moved in with me. It was a bit like the script from *Only Fools and Horses* – me and Joe with 'Uncle Albert' looking after us. Joe and I treated Hunters Oak like a bachelor pad – nights out, women, booze, fast cars, training and playing football.

Good times – full blast.

Joe Allon looked out of the front-room window and saw the beginning of the rest of my life.

He glanced out into the street and said: 'Cor, what a stunner. Come and have a look at this.' I wandered over and saw a woman walking past, and Joe wasn't exaggerating. She was beautiful. Then I did a double-take.

'It's Tanya,' I said. 'I know her. I'd recognise her anywhere.'

* * *

Tanya Lamont was among the kids who used to go to Sunday cricket matches. I went with the Hensard family because Russell's dad played. We were just kids, about twelve, I suppose. Nothing boy/girl about it, just playmates, knocking around together: Russell and me, Tanya and her pal.

Tanya's family are Irish, and she went to Francis Coombe school in Garston but I was at Langleybury and we lost contact. I didn't see her for several years until one night I was in The Three Horseshoes and this girl came up to me and said: 'You're Vincent Jones, aren't you?' I hadn't recognised her, first off. She was beautiful, I certainly recognised that – extremely pretty with long, dark hair. When it dawned on me, we stood and chatted for a while, recalling those cricket matches all that time ago. She also explained that her old man would never let her go to the pub but her mum had agreed on condition that she got back in before her dad. I saw her a couple of times in there and eventually one night decided to ask if I could walk her home.

I had taken my motorbike to the pub, so I left it outside as Tanya and I sauntered back. Nothing too romantic – a cup of tea in the kitchen with her mum. I stayed for the best part of an hour and walked back to the pub. No bloody motorbike! It was the first time I'd had anything nicked.

There was a phone box over the road by the park, so I thought I'd get one of my mates to pick me up, but as I was dialling I saw and heard a bike roaring up and down the park. I walked over and there was a crowd of lads taking it in turns to ride – on my bike.

I saw Tanya in the pub the following week and accused her of setting me up. She insisted she played no part in my bike getting nicked and I did, eventually, believe her. But we did have a fall-out because she said: 'And what about you telling Russell Hensard you got off with me in my house!' What? There hadn't even been a kiss or canoodle. I think Russell was a bit jealous that I'd walked her home so he'd pulled her leg and she didn't see the funny side.

That was it. She blew me out completely and I was sad. There were plenty of women around at the time but she was outstanding. I don't know, there was just something about her, something that made me feel different. I did try to creep back but she wasn't having any of it. If Tanya doesn't like you, she doesn't like you.

We didn't set eyes on one another again until 1984.

It was FA Cup final day, Watford against Everton, and Nigel Callaghan, one of the lads who had gone on to sign pro at Vicarage Road and was matey with Russell, got us two tickets. As we went to park the car, the coach carrying the Watford players' wives and girl-friends breezed past. Another double-take: Tanya was on there.

Russell said to me: 'That's the players' wives' coach and that's Tanya Terry.'

'What are you on about, Tanya Terry?'

'Remember Tanya Lamont, the girl you used to see?' said

Russell. 'Well, that's her, she's married to Steve Terry, Watford's centre half.'

I was quiet for a while and then I saw her again walking up the Wembley steps and I stood and watched her. And she was the most beautiful person I'd ever seen. I thought: 'I wish she was going up those steps to watch me play. I wish I was going out there and that she was married to me.'

A couple of years later there was a piece in the Watford Evening Echo about how Tanya had undergone heart-transplant surgery at Harefield Hospital after complications at the birth of her daughter, Kaley. I read it with mixed emotions – so sad for her that she'd had to suffer something so serious but relieved that she had made a complete recovery.

* * *

It was another of those strange coincidences in my life – unless Granddad had something to do with it. Tanya was now actually living next door but one and I had no idea until I bumped into Tanya's friend Joanne Southern, who'd been at the same school as me. She explained that she and Tanya were living at the house and that Tanya and Steve had split up. Something started jangling in my head.

One night Joe stunned me by saying: 'Hey, I've been round to see Tanya.'

'What do you think you are doing, going round there?'

'There was this rabbit in the road, and next door told me it was the little girl's from the house further on. So I took it round there. Tanya told me it was forever getting out.'

'Well, you can stop being a busy bollocks for a start,' I said, knowing he was winding me up. But it made me think. Tanya and I had been sort of avoiding one another, uneasiness and embarrassment more than anything. A day or two later inspiration struck: ''Course – the rabbit!'

Round I went and knocked on the door. 'Hello, Tanya, it's Vinnie. Do you remember me?'

Yes, she did, and I said, 'It's your rabbit. He was out and I went into the garage and put him in his hutch. You'll have to get that door sorted out.' Then Kaley, who was about four at the time, started crying upstairs, and Tanya said: 'Can you hold on there a minute? I must go up to my little girl.' So I was left at the door and when it blew open slightly with the wind I could see right through into the front room. There was nobody there, so I went in.

I was a bit merry, to be honest. I never lacked confidence, anyway. I put the kettle on, made some coffee, found the biscuits in a drawer and took them through into the main room. When Tanya came down she opened the door, looked outside and thought I'd gone.

'In here. It was freezing out there so I came in and put the kettle on.'

She was really stand-offish. 'Do you always let yourself into other people's houses and put the kettle on?' I could tell she wasn't being the girl I knew from Garston, she was being a bit prim and proper. But we had a coffee and the biscuits and began to talk. We talked and talked right through the night until Kaley woke up: I left at seven the next morning.

Tanya had asked things like 'How did you become a footballer? I thought you were a thug and when I read you were a player I couldn't believe it because I imagined you would be in prison somewhere.' We talked about how she and Steve had grown apart – a bit like Mylene and me – how he had moved in with another girl, and about babies, but she didn't say anything about the heart transplant.

I went home, drove in for training and was back at her house again that afternoon. At weekends a crowd of girls gathered at the house and on summer's evenings I often went round there with Colesy, sitting in the sunshine, chatting and having a great time, and we started going out as a crowd.

Tanya and I were getting to know each other again, growing together, becoming closer but not even holding hands, let alone sealing it with a kiss. There came a day when she said she had to go away for the weekend, to hospital in Nuneaton for laser treatment. It was nothing to do with her heart but serious all the same. It started driving me mad, thinking of her in that hospital so far away. So I asked her friend Mandy to go up there with me.

As usual – whatever predicament she might be in – Tanya had made sure she looked nice. After a little while, Mandy and Tanya's mum, Maureen, left us together. I leaned forward, held Tanya's hands and gave her a kiss. Just a gentle, little one. It was the very first time I'd kissed her.

I had already made up my mind that I was in love with her. I had never felt that way about a girl before. I knew I wanted to be with her and take care of her. When she'd left for the hospital on the Friday I'd gone round to her house and was looking for something when I came across a pile of letters almost as thick as a phone directory. They were bills and many of them were the red variety. I suppose she couldn't cope with them at the time. I wrote cheques for the lot and paid off everything.

Now she looked me in the eyes and said: 'Vinnie, you've got to take me home. Please get the doctor to let me go.' I asked, but the doctor said something that amounted to 'You have to be joking.' He eventually relented when I promised to stay with her.

I picked Tanya up and carried her down the corridors of that hospital and out to the car, laid her in the back, still in her pyjamas, and covered her up with blankets. The car was filled with flowers from her bedside. Back home I waited on her hand and foot while she convalesced.

It was inevitable that I would ask Tanz to marry me. We had just returned home from a night out when I held her calmly and asked: 'Will you marry me? I want to marry you.'

'Yes,' she said. Well, it was more of a shriek and she went crazy about it. That was nice.

'Don't say anything to anybody yet,'

I asked her. 'I want to talk to your dad first. I want to do this properly.'

I rang Tanya's dad, Lou, and asked if I could come round. He thought something was wrong.

'No, nothing's the matter. I just want to come and see you on your own.'

He was alone when I arrived and I just said straight out: 'I want to ask you if I can marry Tanz. She has said yes and I want to ask you for your blessing.'

Lou talked quietly and kindly about Tanya's heart transplant and tried to explain. 'Do you know what you are taking on board? This is a hell of a thing, she's no ordinary girl. We sometimes have panic attacks about it all.'

'I know all that,' I said, 'and I want to look after her for the rest of her life.'

'Then I'm over the moon for you.' And Lou gave me a big hug.

He had never forgotten that I had been there to bring her home early from hospital in Nuneaton. By the time Lou arrived when Tanya had had her transplant operation he wasn't able to enter the ward because of the urgent medical procedures. He desperately wanted to cuddle her, as any father would. He'd been told they weren't sure whether she would make it through the night. Could you imagine, he was standing out in the cold night air when he saw the helicopter bringing Tanya's new heart and only chance of life. I worship the ground Tanz walks on, but that is nothing to what her father thinks of her. He absolutely adores her and is so glad I'm with her, taking care of her.

The worst part for Tanya is the annual check-up, the angiogram she needs at Harefield Hospital. I'm always there and wait outside. It is a major examination and, although she is drugged, she is conscious the whole time. She makes me promise that I'll be there afterwards but the promise isn't necessary. I wouldn't be anywhere else. Sometimes she comes out crying and I just feel: 'This isn't fair – it isn't fair.' It's an immediate reaction to Tanya's discomfort, not a complaint. Harefield is a wonderful place and our gratitude to the experts and staff there cannot be put into words.

Tanya clings to me after those check-ups and I have said to her so many times: 'I'll always be here for you. I'd move mountains.'

To say we live from day to day is wrong because we couldn't exist like that. We make plans for months and months in advance. Tanz's heart collapsed during childbirth, so when it comes round to Kaley's birthday, she does become fragile. You realise it's been another year but there is love and reassurance in our house and we accept that, whether you've got £500 or £5 million, what will be, will be.

I could not imagine being without Tanya now. She's a great kid, terrific personality, beautiful, and when she's on form she just lights up the room. We haven't had many rows but when we've not been talking she'll say, 'Life's too short,' and the making-up is fantastic.

With Tanya on holiday in Mauritius and, below, with her daughter Kaley and puppy!

Chapter 18

Out of a Nightmare, into a Dream

Meeting up with Tanya again, it's a wonder I was able to concentrate on anything, let alone that 1991–92 season with Chelsea.

In fact, we had a pretty good season. Like at Leeds, I enjoyed that feeling of being with a proper football club. There was that strange kind of aura again and I was strutting about with a chest like a cock pigeon. A few feathers were ruffled along the way, of course, not least my own. The FA Cup brought Sheffield United to the Bridge and you're always wound up that little bit tighter playing against a former club. I still find it hard to accept there was time for me to do anything in three seconds but my first move, my first challenge, produced the yellow card from referee Keith Burge's pocket. I was straight in on Dane Whitehouse. I must have been too high, too wild, too strong or too early, because, after three seconds, I could hardly have been too bloody late!

There is another blot on my copybook that I still regard as a joke. Literally, a joke. A £1,500 fine by the FA for 'making obscene gestures to fans' prior to our match against Arsenal at Highbury. I spotted Tony O'Mahoney, my sister's boyfriend, in the crowd, grinned at him, gave him the old sign, jiggling my hand, and

Chelsea v Arsenal, 1991 –
the game during which
I was fined for making
'obscene gestures' to my
friend Tony O'Mahoney.

mouthed: 'You wanker.' Just a spur of the moment joke, to a mate.
But some Arsenal fans made a complaint and I was charged.

We were only a few games into the 1992–93 season when I was
on the move again. Wimbledon, here I come again, for £640,000
or thereabouts. I was gutted to learn that Chelsea were moving
me out.

I had recently fallen out with my agent, Jerome Anderson, over
the notorious *Soccer's Hard Men* video that had me accused of glori-
fying violence and dirty tricks, and was now trying to negotiate my
pay-off at Chelsea. One night I was playing my favourite game,
three-card brag, at my local, The Venture. A bloke was watching us
and after half an hour he introduced himself as Steve Davies and
asked if he could join in.

He sat down next to my old man who warned him:

'Shouldn't get involved in this lot.

It's a bit heavy, mate.'

'That's all right. No problem,' said Steve, who just happened to
be an extremely successful businessman and legal consultant with a

Rolls-Royce out in the car park. Perhaps it was as well, seeing that he ended up losing £800 in that card school and I won the lot.

He came into the pub again the next night and as we chatted it struck me he could help me. I explained about my dispute with Anderson and that I could use some assistance in getting my money from Chelsea and he said he could handle that.

'OK,' I told him, 'you come on board and look after me.' Little did I realise that this chance meeting would develop into such a close and personal friendship in the years to come. I didn't want the problems I'd experienced previously. Some agents spread their loyalty: 'Sorry, Mr Jones is unavailable that day, but Mr so-and-so will be more than happy to oblige.' That kind of thing. I told Steve he could look after me on one condition: that I was his only client. We shook hands on it. Steve was brilliant.

A couple of months later, the shit hit the fan, big-time, about that desperate video. I'd agreed to do it on the understanding that other players would also be talking about their experiences in the game. I never bargained for the way it would come out and the trouble it would cause.

The verbals, the off-the-ball stuff,

studs in the back of the legs.

It was months and months before I heard anything. It turned out that the video had been sold on four or five times from one company to another until some bright spark got hold of it, went to the papers and said: 'Can you believe a professional footballer has come out with this?'

They say 100,000 copies were produced and sold. I never had one, never saw it and wouldn't want one in my home. I wouldn't watch it to this day because I am so ashamed of having been so naive and stupid. The £1,600 I was paid was sent off to a children's charity.

That November I was hauled before the FA disciplinary people. There were about six FA officials confronting me at Lancaster Gate. I'm tempted to say not one of them looked under eighty but that would be wrong: I could be a year or two out. They didn't seem particularly interested in my explanation of how it came about. I told them I had totally disassociated myself from the whole thing, but all they seemed to be saying was that they couldn't afford another such case and had to make an example. They were going to nail me and nail me good. 'Don't condemn me for one bad, bad mistake,' I said. But it was a record £20,000 fine, all the same, plus a six-month ban, suspended for three years.

* * *

Thank heaven Tanya and I had grown so close and that there was a wedding to be planned. The moment Tanya had said yes to marriage I phoned the old man, told him the news and asked him to find me a plot of land. He rang me now to say he'd found a place for us at Redbourn. It was an old derelict shell of a bungalow, part of a farm on a three-acre plot. Straight away, Tanz and I knew it was the place for us. We called it Oaklands and from the front it is virtually an exact replica of Woodlands, the bungalow Dad had bought for the family and done up. I don't know whether I was trying to recreate that home from childhood. I just know that when I saw the plot I thought: 'Woodlands. I want Woodlands right there.'

I did most of the demolition and mucked in with the groundwork. But the builders were held up by heavy snow and I became frustrated because it wasn't happening fast enough. We'd already set a date for the wedding, 25 June 1994, and the frustration began to turn to panic because that very special wedding I had promised Tanya was going to take place in a vast marquee on the field next to the house. We had 100 feet of panelled fencing between the house and the field and the final panel was actually hammered into place at about ten o'clock the night before the ceremony.

My stag night was something else. I went with my pals to Cork for the weekend. Sixty-two of us! There was supposed to be sixty-five but sixty-two turned up, including Dad, Lou, Steve Davies and Wimbledon manager Joe Kinnear, and we had a great time, lots of drinking, leg-pulling and card schools. Steve had sold the whole stag 'do' to the Mirror, stories and pictures right through. But during the final champagne toasts on the Sunday there were a couple of blokes sitting in the hotel with a little camera asking if they could take the odd snap or two. 'Yeah. 'Course. Carry on, boys.' We thought nothing of it, until their pictures appeared in the Star!

There was a group of police with dogs when we arrived back at Stansted. They must have been warned there was a boisterous party

of lads flying in but there was no trouble. They joined in the crack,
managing to smile while the rest of us collapsed as some of the
lads squatted, motionless, on the luggage carousel as it went round
and round, through the exit flaps and back again.

I had explained to Steve about the wedding I wanted. 'If that's
what the boy wants, that's what the boy will have,' he said. And he
helped me to plan it. Steve has a solution for everything. If you want
a pool-cover, he knows where to get one; if you need special lighting or a bouncy castle for a party, ring Steve. He said to leave everything to him, and I did. We had vast marquees, silver service, the
finest food and a helicopter. All in, the wedding cost £100,000.

Steve had sold the wedding to the *News of the World* but word
had got out and when we arrived at the registry office for the official
ceremony on the Friday the place was swarming with press people.
The *News of the World* had left nothing to chance, they must have
had eight or nine blokes there with cardboard shields, thrusting
them in front of the opposition as they tried to get pictures. Tanz
was swamped as she went to get in the car afterwards. Lou hit out
and made sure at least one of them realised we were not to be
messed around. While all this was going on, I legged it out of
the back and was pictured jumping over a wall, leaving my own
wedding!

The press were all over Redbourn as well. We hired a security firm for the Friday and Saturday and it was a good job we did. If ever there was a perfect day on this planet then it was that Saturday Tanya and I were married in front of all our family and friends at our home. You can see the M1 from where we live and there were people, press people, trying to get across the fields and through the woods from the next village.

I asked Johnny Moore to be my best man. There were so many mates I could have chosen, but when it really mattered, when I needed shelter, if you like, Johnny was the one who had taken me in and looked after me. He was delighted to accept. He's very emotional, Johnny, a good crier. My sister Ann was one of the bridesmaids, so was Kaley, with Aaron as a pageboy. I arrived in a helicopter with Johnny – it was lent to us as his wedding present by Kevin Cinamond who has known Tanya all her life.

Tanya didn't show it, but she was in awful pain from one of her feet – a temporary side-effect of the drugs she has to take. She told me later she could hardly put it to the floor on her walk from the house to the marquee, but nobody would have known. When she arrived at my side she looked absolutely sensational. A hell of a lot of tears were shed during that ceremony and the first of them were mine, the second I looked at the stunning lady by my side. The service seemed to fly by and then it was outside to greet all our friends, and the jazz band played right through the meal and on until another couple of hundred guests arrived for the disco in the evening: a black-tie do.

Wisey, John Barnes, Sam Hammam, Stanley Reed, the Wimbledon chairman, and Joe Kinnear were all there. Howard Wilkinson was away but Mick Hennigan came and so did Frenchy. Joe Allon was among nine ushers. Some of my mates, like the Bedmond boys, had never worn evening dress before. It was great to see them all done up – Moss Bros must have had a field day! I did my party piece, getting up to sing 'Woolly Bully', and the bride and groom began the dancing by being first on the floor to 'Where Do You Go To My Lovely?' – our favourite song. I sang a little to my wife during that dance – 'When you go on your summer vacation, you go to Juan Les Pins …' And that's exactly where we went for our honeymoon.

A week away was long enough for both of us. I can't remember

the last time we were away for a two-week holiday. We like being at home, with the kids around and the animals. Both of us value our home-life more than anything. As we turned into the driveway I noticed the electronic doors to the garage were closed. Tanya's friend Mandy, later our housekeeper for a time, ran out of the house with Maureen, asked if we'd enjoyed ourselves – and then up went the doors. The garage was packed. All our families and friends were there again – or maybe they hadn't left after the wedding! Drinks, a fantastic buffet. Everybody sat around while Tanz and I opened the presents and then watched the wedding on video. It was the perfect finish to a beautiful wedding. I was determined that Tanya should have the best.

All the bouquets were handed to the grandparents – and we have quite a few, between us. I had a cuddle with my nan and whispered: 'It's a shame my granddad isn't here.'

'Oh, but he is, Vinnie.'

'Yeah, I know he is, really. I know.'

* * *

I have a real glow now, about the family being so close. I look back on the break-up, all those years ago, and can see it in a different light. It hurt as a kid but you grow up to realise that these things happen and it is wrong to lay blame.

Tanya and I cannot have children together, but I have a beautiful boy, she has a beautiful girl and we both regard them as our own. Tanya gets on well with Mylene, and Steve Terry often brings his kids to our house to splash around in the pool with Kaley and Aaron. In fact, while the children stay at the house, Steve and I have a day out. There is no awkward atmosphere when we all meet up, and that's the way it should be. As long as Tanya is happy and the kids are happy, then I'm content.

The day I officially adopted Kaley meant so much to me. Mylene hasn't married and Aaron remains Aaron Jones, living in St Albans about ten minutes away. Tanz and I wanted Kaley to go to private school and I said I didn't want her facing questions about why her name was Terry yet her mum's was Jones. Kaley agreed and Steve was in favour.

Kaley wanted to be part of the family and that made me feel

The happy couple outside one of the huge marquees.

proud. I pay her fees at Abbots Hill and Aaron's at St Columbus Preparatory School in St Albans and I like the thought of the children getting private education. I don't look on it as a status symbol for me and Tanz, but I sometimes allow myself to think 'The children are getting the best education. I can't have done everything wrong in my life.' I don't want my kids hanging around the estates. I don't have knowledge about classic plays and opera and so on, but I would like them to be interested in such things. I can't personally give them that kind of knowledge but I've put myself in a situation where I can make it available to them.

I have to confess to spoiling them, especially Kaley, who is at home with us. I think I've made her more worldly. I've taught her to drive my Land Rover and she's had just about every animal on God's earth, although she does suffer badly from an allergy to fur. We went to buy her a white pony but the same thing happened that occurs if ever the dogs manage to sneak upstairs and lie on her bed – her face puffs up as if she's just been hit by Mike Tyson. I was brought up streetwise but always interested and involved with animals. I don't know whether it will be possible, but my ambition for Kaley is that she should become a vet.

A pal of mine from Leeds recently met Aaron for the first time in years. He was tickled pink and rang his wife to say: 'You would never believe this is Vinnie's boy, sitting here. He sounds so posh.' Never mind about posh – if he speaks properly, that's brilliant. His mum has the job of keeping an eye on him, making sure he does his homework, but when he comes here, he lets his hair down, puts his overalls on and just has a great time. He and Kaley behave like any brother and sister. They fight like brother and sister and love each other like brother and sister.

And we're all extremely proud of the pair of them.

Three generations of Joneses: me, my son Aaron and father Peter.

My beautiful bride Tanya, with Aaron and Kaley.

Chapter 19

This is Your Captain Speaking

My move back to Wimbledon had come out of the blue, as most transfers do. I was hurt – yeah, properly hurt – to be told Chelsea had accepted a bid for me. I knew they were wanting to bring in Nigel Spackman so when Chelsea managing director Colin Hutchinson rang me I dug my heels in: 'No way, Col. I love it at Chelsea.'

About half an hour later, Hutchinson had doubled the money but I repeated, 'Col, there's no way. I'll only talk to them if you get me all my dough.' I knew in my heart that I should have stayed at Chelsea to improve my status as a player, but when I took another call to be told a deal had been done with Chelsea and Wimbledon each paying me £80,000, I went and met Joe Kinnear for the first time. There was the lure of being back with Sam and the boys, and the fact that Joe wanted me as skipper. Sure, I do like to be wanted – don't we all? But my wallet ruled my head as well. The deal was colossal and it gave me a stature, financially, I hadn't known before.

I immediately took to Joe Kinnear, who I found to be a tremendous fella, and nothing has happened since to lessen my affection for him. There was outrage in the newspapers. How can Vinnie

Jones be captain of a Premiership side? But Joe never once batted an eyelid. 'He's my captain and our leader,' he told them all and it was clear, from the start, that we'd hit it off. I had found not only a manager but also a new mate who I knew would be completely honest with me. He gave me responsibility and I loved it. Even though Dave Kemp and Lawrie Sanchez were doing the coaching, I was the third coach in line and had the respect of all the players. It was difficult during the first weeks, though, because there were players who had become established in their own right, like Robbie Earle and Warren Barton. I had never played with them and I think the return of one of the 'originals' put a few noses out of joint.

I had to be strong, acknowledge that they had succeeded in keeping Wimbledon rolling, but I also needed to make it clear that I was there to do a job. Fash was still there, as was Hans Segers, but there were quite a few up and coming members of the 'gang' and we soon became matey and settled things down.

The Crazy Gang element and influence, the high jinks, had been maintained at Wimbledon although not on the scale of the earlier days. There was still that keen collective spirit among us and a protective quality that saw us close ranks whenever one of us was in trouble. We got along fine with the sports writers generally; it was the news journalists who had to be kept at bay. On many occasions we discovered a group of them waiting at the training ground and Joe would pull me over to ask: 'Who's in the shit this time?' There were two routines: 'Slip him out of the back before the end of training,' Joe would say. 'Leave his car keys and we'll get one of the boys to run it back for him.' Or the alternative was for Joe to call the reporters together saying: 'Good morning, how can we help you?' as half a dozen of us wearing balaclavas and armed with buckets of water roared from the dressing-rooms and soaked the lot of them. When, later, they protested about damaged cameras and equipment, Sam would explain that it was a group of youth players who seemed to have been involved but nobody was quite sure of their identities. He would deal with it if they could tell him who they were!

In December of 1994 Wimbledon had a new international footballer among their ranks – Vincent Peter Jones of Wales! There had been talk of my qualifying for the Republic of Ireland when Big Jack Charlton was looking for somebody who might do a job at

centre half. Nanny Harris, Mum's mother, was born in Dublin but despite our efforts to trace a birth certificate it was like looking for a needle in a haystack because, apparently, many records had been destroyed years earlier in a fire. The Welsh national side was having a bad time and somebody wrote an article saying they could do with Vinnie Jones in midfield. Steve Davies did his homework and, although I was a bit reluctant at first, he eventually traced Granddad Arthur Jones's birth certificate. It had to be submitted in time for me to join the squad for the European Championship qualifying game against Bulgaria in Cardiff. But it so nearly all went wrong.

The documentation had to be completed and delivered to meet the rules. It was agreed that somebody from the Welsh FA should sort out the paperwork, and the plan was for me to set off the next morning and drive to Cardiff. I was instructed not to drive over the Severn Bridge before we'd had the official nod.

My phone rang at about two o'clock in the morning. It was Steve. 'Do you realise, boy, we've made all that effort to get this done and we've left it to someone else to actually sort out the procedure in time. What happens if they don't do it?'

'Good shout. So what do we do?'

'I'm not leaving anything to chance. I'm going to get down to Cardiff, right now.'

He arrived in Cardiff in time for an early breakfast and waited and waited for the bloke who was supposed to be sorting out my details. Ten o'clock … twenty-past … half-past … nothing and nobody. Steve phoned the guy and found he was in a meeting elsewhere.

Meanwhile, somewhere on the M4, I had cut my speed but I was getting close to the Severn Bridge. Down to 35 mph and slowing! Finally the call came through.

'You are there, son. You are there. It's all done. You can get yourself over that bridge.'

I had had the words to 'Land of My Fathers' in Welsh on tape for some time and played them over and over in the car wherever I had been driving. I had learned it phonetically – well, most of it, anyway. Certainly enough of it to be able to ring Steve, once I'd crossed the Severn, and sing it to him full blast.

Even when I was driving down there, it still seemed unreal. Me playing for Wales. I'd come through an awful lot, even to win the

Previous pages
Top left: My return to Wimbledon, as captain, in 1992.

Bottom left: One of those all-too-familiar Vinnie v referee moments – Crystal Palace v Wimbledon.

Right: Psyching myself up.

right to play professionally, so the thought of international recognition still wasn't making much sense in my head. Over lunch on the day of the match the boys were asking me if I'd brought my passport and I reckoned I was the victim of a wind-up. Until I went to board the coach and saw a right old commotion. A lot of shaking heads and frowning faces.

'What's going on?' I asked.

'It's Mark Hughes – he's forgotten his passport.'

I pulled Mike Smith, the manager, aside and told him, very sheepishly: 'Mike, I haven't got my passport with me, either.'

He said only two words: 'F … ing hell.'

Unknown to me at the time, and probably to most people reading this, every player on the team sheet for an international game, home or away, has to produce his passport. Without it, you cannot play. FIFA rules. After all that it looked as if I was going to miss out because I didn't have my passport for a match in Wales.

'Sparky' and I boarded the coach anyway, but it still looked grim when we reached the stadium. Officials running in all directions, including the referee, but the rule book looked like winning. Thankfully, common sense won the day. I'm sure Hughesy was more important to Wales than I was and I felt certain something would be done to make sure he didn't miss the game. They took an instamatic photograph of the pair of us, stamped it and we signed it and dated and timed it, as well as arranging for copies of our passport details to be faxed. Luckily, the referee accepted it but I've no doubt that Sparky forgetting his passport was the biggest stroke of luck I had with Wales.

It was so important to me, that first appearance. For Granddad's sake. He had been born in a workhouse in Wales but lived in Watford with Nanny Ann when I was a kid. We were all mad Watford fans and he used to have his own little patch on the corner of Shrodells, opposite the directors' box and named after the hospital where I was born.

Being Welsh, though, Granddad's main passion was his rugby. He also enjoyed a little bet from time to time on the horses and the dogs and it's no coincidence that, like him, I now own a racing greyhound.

I didn't ask Granddad for his help before that first game for Wales. It was enough for me just to be there. All I had to do was step out on that pitch and hear the sound of the first whistle and I was an international footballer. I sang the Welsh national anthem as loudly as I could before the kick-off against Bulgaria and I knew that Granddad would be watching and feeling extremely proud.

I know people have a laugh and a joke about it, but it hurts me when they say that I'm as much Welsh as a rarebit. I have no time for people like that because I feel Welsh and regard myself as Welsh. I haven't known many prouder moments in my life. What is it they say, pride comes before a fall? It did in my case.

It was in Cardiff again, a night game in June 1995, another European Championship qualifier, this time against Georgia. I had started off soundly with good, clean tackles, winning the headers, passing the ball well. Suddenly it was as if my heart and my guts overruled my head. There was this feeling that everything was going my way and I could do anything at all. I clattered into Mikhail Kavelachvili. He went down in front of me and I trampled all over him. He was on the floor as if he'd been shot. I couldn't argue at being sent off but it might not have been more than a caution if the bloke hadn't reacted like that. As soon as I was red-carded he was up again and flying. But although there was no intent to hurt the guy I knew I was doing something I shouldn't. By the time you fully realise it, in the heat of the action, it is too late and you are staring at the red card.

That was my worst ever sending-off. Wales were a sort of early-days Wimbledon – striving against the odds, always seeming to be up against it – and I had been honoured with a place in their team. And had let everybody down. And then, to lose 1–0 with only ten men – I was made to feel even bloody worse.

It cost me a five-match suspension and, in the meantime, Bobby Gould was installed as the new manager of Wales. As soon as I heard, I feared my international days were numbered, if not over. Some of the other players argued I would be OK because he was my mate and I tried to tell them that we weren't that close – Gouldy and I had had more wars than love affairs. And yet Bobby was to give me the opportunity to do something precious few footballers, not even some of the truly great players, have ever done.

It was in Holland and the usual skipper, Barry Horne, was out injured.

At the hotel Gouldy announced: 'Look, the fairest way to do this

A proud moment: captaining Wales in their match against Holland in a World Cup qualifier in 1996.

is for me to leave it to you. You are all men. Just write your own choice as skipper. That includes putting your own name on paper if you think you should be skipper.' I put down my own name and I think one or two others did the same. But when the manager read out from the slips of paper it was: 'Vinnie Jones … Vinnie Jones … Vinnie Jones.' I was voted captain of Wales by secret ballot!

I don't think Bobby was expecting it. I wasn't part of his equation. In fact, when the result was clear, I swear I heard him sigh: 'Oh no.' But there was a spontaneous round of applause from the players. I ran straight upstairs, rang Steve Davies and said: 'You'll never guess what's happened.'

'You've been made captain.'

'How do you know?'

'Because,' he said, 'your story just never ends.'

Now all those people who argued that I should never have been an international footballer had to say I certainly shouldn't have been an international captain. And I had beaten the lot of them.

Welsh recognition warranted another tattoo, a third to complete the set, and I had a beauty put on my chest – the dragon and the feathers. It took three hours and cost £150. But after nine caps my international career ended almost as abruptly as it began. Bobby made it clear he was going to rebuild the team and, although he retained some of the older players, he put me on stand by. No explanation, not even a phone call. The first I knew was when the press contacted me. I still haven't heard from him. I do think he should have called me and explained.

I nearly picked up the phone and rang him, and realise now that I should have done. Who knows? I might have ended up as his No 2 with the international side.

Chapter 20

Without a doubt, 15 February 1995 was a black day in the history of English football. It marked the terrible occasion when the international match between Terry Venables' England and Jack Charlton's Republic of Ireland had to be abandoned after twenty-seven minutes because of rioting by visiting yobs who called themselves supporters. It was also the night when I did something that almost had the gravest consequences.

I was sent out to Dublin to write a piece for my column in the *News of the World*. We were staying at Jury's Hotel, only a short walk from the Lansdowne Road ground. We grabbed our coats to leave for the stadium about a couple of hours before kick-off but there was quite a crowd of boisterous Irish supporters outside, big fellas who were keen to let me know they hadn't exactly welcomed the thought of me playing for their country. They had obviously read of our attempts to try to establish my qualification, even though I was in the Wales team by then.

There were one or two provocative comments – the only time I've ever had any stick from the Irish – and Steve rightly decided it was unwise to run the gauntlet. So we stayed in the bar, settled in front of the box and were appalled, like everybody else, when those idiots following England started breaking up the seats and hurling their missiles from the stand after the Irish team had scored.

It wasn't long before everybody was back at the hotel, supporters and loads of press men frantically milling around, doing their stories. We were sitting having a bottle of champagne when a bloke came over and said somebody wanted to meet me. I went across, there was a bit of fooling around and everybody knows what happened then. Ted Oliver, a news reporter from the Mirror, was sitting at a table with a few other people. I'd had a good drink – I wasn't 'steaming', but I was in high spirits. Oliver said something quite innocuous really but I felt he was belittling me. Then there was a bit of grabbing and tugging, so I got his head in my arm and took hold of his nose with my teeth.

It was completely in jest.

Unfortunately, I didn't realise my own strength. Perhaps I got carried away with the drink to some extent. That was it, he told me to clear off and I went back to my friends. Next minute, somebody came over and said: 'You've bit his nose.' I went to apologise to Oliver and found him pressing his nose with a white handkerchief that had some blood on it, but I still didn't realise that it was quite serious.

'Bloody hell,' I said, 'I'm sorry.'

Some time later, on my way to bed, I spotted him having a drink and went over again. 'Look, I am sorry about what happened.' But I wasn't able to make any progress, so I went to bed.

At Stansted Airport the next morning I walked into chaos. There were media people everywhere. I looked behind me wondering who the hell was on our plane, then I was swamped as somebody yelled: 'You bit off a bloke's nose in Ireland.'

The word was that I'd amputated his bloody nose. I was straight on the phone to Tanya and she was crying. I was saying, 'I haven't done what they're saying, it wasn't like that, it was nothing,' and explaining that I hadn't phoned earlier because I'd caught the early flight, but she was terribly upset. There were cameras and reporters at the house, and radio and TV people constantly on the phone.

I got home and gave Tanya a cuddle, and the sight of her so

distressed made me cry as well. I just went upstairs and lay on the bed. I couldn't cope with everything that was happening around me. It wasn't a nervous breakdown as such, but it was some sort of emotional collapse, I suppose. My mouth was wide open, my eyes staring into space and I couldn't move. I couldn't feel my legs or any part of my body. I was gone, wasted. What on earth was happening to Vinnie Jones?

Steve came upstairs and sat with me and held my hand and told me to get myself together, that Tanya would be up with a cup of tea in a minute. But I just thought: 'This is it. This is the end of the world.' They left me alone but must have checked periodically, because Steve has since told me I was lying in the foetal position, sucking my thumb.

I had always faced and handled everything before. Always held up my hands for whatever I'd done. This time, I couldn't. There was me thinking that what happened in Ireland had been nothing more than a bit of horseplay that got a little rough, yet I found myself being pursued as if I had murdered somebody. I must have lain there for about four hours. Then I felt freezing cold, icy from head to toe even though the central heating was on. Sweat poured off me. I forced myself off the bed, came downstairs and found Steve still there. I was in a daze, just moping around.

There was worse to come, next day. A great deal worse. I was up at 6am and went straight to the shop to fetch the papers. I braced myself for the worst. And there it was, splashed all over the front page of the Mirror – 'Mirrorman's soccer riot agony' – with a picture of Oliver and his damaged hooter. Inside the paper there were more pictures and the heading 'Vinnie fixed me with his teeth and shook me like a dog with a dead rabbit'.

Although I was expecting to be the centre of controversy yet again, I didn't anticipate the story being given quite that kind of treatment. Coming as it did alongside all the aftermath of the violence at Lansdowne Road, the timing could not have been worse. It wasn't long before reporters descended on the house again and the phone rang continuously. I decided to go in for training. Often it is a tremendous help just to get in there among the other players, hear their reassurances, put up with their leg-pulling and get out into the fresh air and run and run. That day, though, the press were there before I was and I had one eye constantly on the car park, wondering who and how many were going to turn up.

Steve had been in regular touch with the *News of the World*. Sports editor Mike Dunn had said it looked as if the editor, Piers Morgan, was going to sack me, believing he would be ridiculed by the newspaper industry if he continued to publish my column. Eventually, we seemed to settle on a compromise. Piers Morgan demanded that I should do my side of the story with a photograph suitably confirming my regret while, at the same time, offering my own version of events, putting it all into some perspective and pointing out that 'it takes two to tango'. That is exactly what I did and I believed the problem with the *News of the World*, at least, had been resolved.

I was still uneasy, though. The longer I thought about it the more worried I became that the *News of the World* would have a change of mind that wouldn't exactly be to my advantage. I began to feel awful again. I went upstairs and back to my bed and Tanya tells me I was in an even worse state than the day before. I was back in that half curled-up position, unable to concentrate on any particular thought, unable to clear my head of the turmoil and the pressure that squeezed and squeezed the longer the day went on.

Then the answer struck me.

Steve was downstairs with Vince Needham, another of my friends. Vince, looking concerned, suggested: 'Come on, boy. Let's go and have a pint.'

'No,' I said. 'I'll stay here. I need to settle down a bit. Clear my head. Don't worry – I'm going to be all right.'

I persuaded Steve and Vince to go and reassured them again that everything would be OK. Then there was Tanz.

'I've got to have something to eat, love,' I said to her. 'Can you go down to the shops and get me something? I'll be fine. I'm going to have a bath.'

She agreed, but I recognised heartbreak written all over her face. I remember thinking, 'She has found herself married to a monster. I am a monster.' Those who get to know me always say the same thing, that I'm really a nice bloke, soft-hearted and generous, but in our house at that moment I felt like the thug others had portrayed. I thought: 'What am I doing to this beautiful woman? I can't keep doing these things to her.'

I had made up my mind what I was going to do, but wanted to say goodbye to Tanya without raising her suspicions in any way. Before she left I held her tight, kissed her and said: 'Look, I love you. You are everything in my life.' I went to the window and watched her go. Then I put my shoes on, went and unlocked the cabinet and took down my twenty-bore shotgun, loaded it and walked out of the house.

With the gun under my arm I walked up the path and headed for the wood at the back of the house. It was a terrible early evening – dark, bitterly cold and it was spitting with rain as I lowered my head against a strong, biting wind. I knew exactly where I was going. There was a little spot in the corner of the wood where I used to go pigeon shooting. I had my own little seat, an old oil-drum, and I was going to sit there and put the gun barrel in my mouth …

Suddenly, out of nowhere, Tessie, my little Jack Russell, came bounding up to me. Then she went hopping and skipping all over the place. She distracted my attention, and I must have stood and watched her for between five and ten minutes. It began to change my mood. The madness began to fall into place and the threat of it receded. I thought: 'Out here, just me with my dog, there's not a lot anybody can do to me. If I do what I came to do a lot of people might be happy. But it will break my wife's heart.' It could well have killed Tanya, too.

I thought of Tanz returning from the shops and coming and finding me. I couldn't do it knowing what I would do to her. I turned round, walked back, went into the garage, removed the cartridges and put the gun back in the cabinet.

It was about a month later that I told her what I had planned that day. She said: 'Whatever happens, whatever we have to go through from now on, never, ever contemplate doing that.' I promised her there would never be any repeat. And we both broke down in tears.

There has definitely been a change in me since that weekend. I think I have spent too much time and effort fighting other people's battles or, at least, believing I needed to go steaming in on their behalf. I came to realise that part of life was about me as well. I've had players come to live with me when they were in trouble, without a pot to piss in. They were very grateful at the time, living rent free, and when they left I never heard from them again. I thought of those people, those kinds of things, how I thought it was all down to me to try to keep the Wimbledon spirit going, but now I decided: 'Let it take care of itself. If it's that important, the other lads will keep it going. It's not down to me alone.'

If I wasn't married to Tanz I think I could still take everything on the chin without a problem. I wouldn't have calmed down or grown up as much. But breaking her heart breaks my heart into even more pieces. I have to remember what my wife went through and that she is on medication, so I can't afford to put her through such things.

Wimbledon were due to play a Cup tie at Liverpool on the Sunday and I travelled with them for the overnight stay in Warrington on the Saturday. I had gathered myself together a bit by then and was sure I was going to be able to play. About nine o'clock I took a telephone call from Steve.

'Jonah? We've got trouble.'

'What now?'

'Just had a call from the News of the World – Piers Morgan's sacked you.'

It was like somebody booting me right in the pit of the stomach. I went to see Kinnear again and his response said a lot for his professionalism.

'Listen,' he said, 'we've had this for three days, now. You've got to be honest with me, Vinnie. Are you going to be able to play tomorrow?'

I was sure I was going to be OK. Until I went to my room and tried to sleep, and couldn't. I didn't get a wink throughout that night. I went to see Joe and Sam Hammam first thing on the Sunday morning and told them: 'I'm sorry, but I'm no good to you today.'

Sam passed me the keys to his green Volvo and I drove straight home to Tanya.

The News of the World ran my version of the Dublin story – together with a picture of me, head in hands. But they also ran one right across the back page announcing they had sacked me. They did pay me for my piece and, as far as I recall, settled any outstanding payments. Not that Piers Morgan and I remained at loggerheads. Funny, but when he later became editor of the Mirror he actually took me on again as a columnist.

I never went back to those woods. I feared that if I did my mind might change again. I could have pulled the trigger. Or I could have said, 'Sod football and everybody in it – I'm going gamekeeping and I'll read about myself in twenty years when somebody does a feature in a newspaper wondering whatever happened to Vinnie Jones.' Or I could scramble out of the brambles, face the world again and get on with it and win back some credit and respect. That's what I decided to do.

Chapter 21

Moving On

Despite my conscious decision to let some things take their course without my involvement, the old competitive instincts survived. That fierce will to win and the resentment of anything that struck me as an injustice never left me and probably never will.

In December 1995 the eleventh red card of my career was waved at me by Dermot Gallagher. This sending-off was to become infamous because of the remarks I made about foreign players and the FA 'disrepute' charge that followed. It was a wet pitch at Stamford Bridge, really slippery, and I expected Gallagher to make allowances for the conditions. He didn't. In the fourteenth minute, when I went in on Dan Petrescu, he booked me. The match had only been resumed ten minutes or so when I challenged Ruud Gullit near the corner flag. Admittedly I went in from behind, but I did also get a touch on the ball. The big Dutchman went over in a heap and I thought his reaction was excessive, to say the least. However, we ended up winning the match 2–1 – a terrific result for Wimbledon.

I was still wound up about that red card when I returned home to find a couple of press lads sitting outside the house. They'd been tipped off that I'd had a go at Gullit, verbally, on my way off. In the heat of the moment I opened up, so the next day – wallop! A big show in the paper with me complaining about foreign players 'squealing like pot-bellied pigs'. If I had thought longer, considered it in quieter moments, I could have made my case without particularly offending anybody.

I felt, and still do feel, that a lot of foreign players roll over more than they have cause to and make too much of the slightest touch. My opinion was valid but I expressed it emotionally and too colourfully for the liking of the people who run the game. Diving and suchlike are condemned by managers and players one minute, but the same people rejoice when somebody in their team does it and gets a penalty the following week. I once gave Detsi Kruszynski, my own team mate, a right bollocking for rolling over and over when he didn't need to and the opposing fans loved me for it. I think it's great when referees book the divers and the ones who feign or exaggerate injury. There are still too many cases of double standards applied in English football. The same with agents. Managers and directors say they detest agents – until the value of the agent suits them and their cause.

People are not honest enough sometimes. Managers, players, referees, all of us. Even journalists, because when they see these double standards, they should hammer them, too. It shouldn't all be left to the referee, who has enough problems to cope with already. I know it is part of the culture overseas, but that doesn't mean we should condone it and see these cheating antics creeping into the English game and being copied by our own players.

The 1996–97 season saw Wimbledon in reach of Wembley again. The low point of the season for me was the day of the semi-final against Chelsea at Highbury. We stayed the night before at a hotel that didn't suit us. I'm not looking for excuses, but nothing seemed to feel right. We were a bit like Liverpool the night before we beat them in the FA Cup final. John Barnes has often said that they felt slightly bored, a little bit niggly; flat, with no buzz about the place. And now, nine years later, the same thing was happening to Wimbledon.

I spoke to Granddad. 'Just be with us. Please get us through it.'

But even that was different. I sensed that he, for once, was saying to me: 'You can't just get in touch and ask me to go and buy you a lottery ticket.' I felt as though I was being tested, and the feeling stayed with me all the way to Highbury on the coach, during the warm-up and in the dressing-room before the game.

We were all crap.

I can't explain why, but we didn't have a run in us – any of us. The preparation had been superb, the approach to the game had been great. Joe had given everybody the chance to be flying that day but we never looked like raising our game. We started off by managing to row among ourselves. Chelsea set off with Roberto Di Matteo as a forward midfield player and we began by bollocking Oyvind Leonhardsen because he wouldn't sit in and do the job that was expected. He eventually knuckled down and we didn't do too badly for a while, but the inevitable outcome was nailed down by a brilliant goal from Gianfranco Zola and another from 'Sparky' Hughes.

Back in the dressing-room we knew we had all let ourselves down. There was no ranting or raving. Even at the end of the game we couldn't get ourselves worked up. That was unheard of: Wimbledon, of all teams, sitting on a coach having been ninety minutes from Wembley and not able to get upset about losing. It

Successfully tackling the Brazilian player Juninho in an encounter with Middlesbrough in 1995.

I scored the only goal of the game to beat Arsenal in 1997.

All smiles as the Dons
go through to the semi-
finals of the FA Cup in
1997.

was something I will never be able to explain.

The next season was to be my last with Wimbledon and once
again we were among the favourites for relegation. I was one of
several people at Selhurst Park who had a feeling we were in for a
difficult time. As things turned out, Wimbledon were to survive and
I found myself involved in a struggle for survival one division lower,
having moved to Queens Park Rangers, who needed vital points
from a few remaining matches.

Of course my departure from Wimbledon left a lump in my
throat for a while, but I believed that going to Loftus Road as player-
coach was a great move for me, offering me the chance to learn the
ropes of management before eventually becoming the gaffer in my
own right. When I signed I was told: 'Look, we're in the shit. We
need a couple of strong men, sound characters in the side. We've a
chance of getting Neil Ruddock on loan and think that with you in
the middle we should just about scrape through.' Thankfully, QPR
survived in the First Division.

Manager Ray Harford was good enough to say to me: 'You pick
my brains. However long it takes, I'll teach you all I can.' I had no
hesitation. Ray is a man's man – I like everything about him. I had
visions of standing up there alongside him and being part of a successful partnership on the lines of Brian Clough and Peter Taylor,
Joe Kinnear and Terry Burton, Howard Wilkinson and Mick
Hennigan, Don Howe and Bobby Gould.

The dread of being finished in football, of ending my career as a
player with nothing else on the horizon, became as intense as my
fear of dying. With every week that had passed at Wimbledon, the
more I had come to believe I would have to stay in football for the
sake of my life and soul. I had spent all those years there learning
the true value of collective spirit and of having the will to beat the
odds. But that club just had to stay in the top division if they were to
remain in business. At least, that was the feeling around the place. It
was as if we were in the middle of the Atlantic Ocean clinging to a
plank of wood, and if we ever let go of it we would drown. I felt that
if they did go down I'd have to finish playing altogether.

If I hadn't become a player, or if I had looked beyond gamekeeping for a living, I would have joined the army. I need people around
me. I have to be the one organising things. I often thought that if
ever I became disenchanted with the game, or it rejected me, I

In the dugout as coach
of QPR in a pre-season
friendly against Spurs,
1998.

would like to get up my own game farm. But, once I'd graduated from player-coach, football management it was – or so I thought.

* * *

I put my money into property, whereas most players put theirs into pensions. I've bought houses for Nanny Ann, in Abbots Langley, and for Tanya's nan, Ella. Mum, Dave and my sister live in a house I own down the road in Hemel Hempstead and the one next door but one is mine as well. I've bought my sister two or three cars over the years, and Dad has had a Jeep. I transfer money into my nan's account every month plus any odd cheques, here and there, and spent about £20,000 doing her house up for her.

We moved to Boxmoor in July 1998. There I was, technically two years away from official retirement, spending heavily on a new house. There was an unfortunate story behind the move from Oaklands: difficulties with the neighbours. I had never before experienced the combination of depression and fear that grabbed hold of me during and after the court case that followed my bust-up with next-door neighbour Timothy Gear. One night in the police cells after my arrest was bad enough, but what followed was a total nightmare.

I was always sure I would be cleared of the charges – actual bodily harm and criminal damage – and that was my feeling throughout the two-day hearing at St Albans Magistrates Court at the beginning of June. When the magistrates retired to make up their minds, even one of the policemen involved in the case said to me: 'You must be very confident of the outcome.' But whatever you feel, in those circumstances, you can never be certain of anything.

The magistrates, a man and two women, were out for about a couple of hours, although for me it seemed more like a couple of weeks. It must have been a pretty close call. I was worried as the time dragged by, but there was also the reassuring feeling that, apart from the verdict, nothing bad could happen to me immediately. There wouldn't be a sentence there and then, so whatever the decision, at least I would be going home that day. That knowledge softened the blow quite a bit when the magistrates came back into court and announced that they had found the charges proved.

It was the next stage that drove me crackers. We were moving to

Boxmoor on 1 July, and I was due to return to the court the next day. So I had a month to wait before learning of my fate. I was trying to put a brave face on it, but I was becoming convinced that they were going to put me away.

I knew I could have coped with prison. People who have done time have told me, 'The first night is the worst. After that it's all right.' I would have adjusted to the routine and got on with it. I might even have come to enjoy parts of it. That's me: I muck in and make the most of any given circumstances.

But it wasn't about me alone. It was about Tanya and the kids and the rest of the family, who I knew would stand by me. It was about the people at Queens Park Rangers, who had made me assistant manager. I spoke to chairman Chris Wright and chief executive Clive Berlin. They both said they were fully behind me but I couldn't be sure exactly what that meant.

I drank more in those weeks than I have ever done in my life. I seemed to live at The Steamcoach in Hemel Hempstead with the boys. I was drinking for company, drinking to forget. And I did forget for a while, but only for as long as the effect of the booze lasted. Back home I would sit and read a newspaper or magazine without consciously taking in a word of it. I'd stare at the television without seeing what was on the screen. Even in the comfort of my own home, I was frightened.

We arrived at Boxmoor for our first night in our new house knowing that it could be my last night there for months. Hardly the time for a party. Instead we trooped off to court again on 2 July. The same little group of family and friends offering reassuring words to one another but with me still fearing the worst, feeling that anything less would be a fantastic relief, and for some reason thinking to myself, as I always do: 'Whatever happens in my life, something good always comes out of it.'

I stood next to my solicitor, Mr Reid. He was addressing the bench, talking about my personal circumstances, my job and so on when the chairman of the magistrates leaned forward and said quietly: 'Mr Reid, we are not considering a custodial sentence.'

When I heard those few words I disappeared. It was as if I just floated away. It was no longer me, Vinnie Jones, standing there in that courtroom. It was just my empty suit – I had dropped out of it through the trouser legs. I daren't look at anybody, not even at

Tanya or my sister. I was fixed to the spot, elated but frightened to death to move a muscle or show any kind of facial expression. Yet I knew that any punishment they were to hand out now would be completely acceptable. It turned out to be 100 hours of community service, with a fine and costs amounting to £1,150. Apart from the conviction itself, the stain on my record, the worst outcome of the court case was the loss of my shotguns, which had been confiscated by the police on the night of my arrest.

Afterwards we took our legal team back to Boxmoor and drank champagne. Then we had a late lunch at The Steamcoach, where Steve Davies put £500 behind the bar and the phone never stopped ringing. All my old mates arrived, and I spent virtually all of the Thursday, Friday, Saturday and Sunday there.

I had hoped I could do my community service coaching kids, possibly under-privileged kids. I thought there would be a decent chance of it, seeing as that was how Eric Cantona fulfilled his punishment for his 'Kung-fu' dust-up with the bloke who had bad-mouthed him at Selhurst Park. But the probation officer picked me up from the house, took me to an old people's home and told me: 'This is what you will be doing. The place needs decorating.' That was my task – painting, Sundays and Wednesdays.

I was devastated when I heard suggestions that it would be 'inappropriate' or 'unsuitable' for me to help children. That hurt, particularly as I have done so much for needy children, and am proud of being a patron of SPARKS, Sports Aid Research Charity for Kids. There was also a dispute after a mysterious note was put through my letterbox by a woman asking me to get in touch because, she said: 'You should know what's going on.' Steve rang her to be told: 'Look, I've been pressured into giving information to the probation office dealing with Vinnie's case. They're allegedly tipping off the papers about where he's doing his work. I'm getting very scared and I want out.'

A picture of me painting appeared in the Mirror. Steve and I were amazed at hearing all this. The police became involved and two women were arrested. I felt betrayed. I had done one day of service. In the circumstances, I thought the whole thing had to be reviewed. Even though Tanya, Steve and I had all given statements to the police, and a woman from the probation office had been sacked, I was taken back to court and accused of breaching my

Michael Barrymore and me meeting some of the winners of the Woman's Own Millennium Children of Courage Awards, 1999.

community service. It all seemed so insensitive – it ran up more expense, as well, involving solicitors and a barrister – especially as, on the three occasions I was accused of not turning up for my community service, my solicitor had informed them why I would be absent. Nevertheless they found me guilty on two of the three counts and extended my community service by forty hours, from 100 to 140, and charged me all the costs.

My solicitor told me: 'We'll appeal against the extra forty hours. Get as much under your belt as you can before we go back to court.' I actually completed ninety-one hours before the appeal.

Back in court in St Albans, we objected to one of the magistrates because of local authority connections. We succeeded, but it took all day, by which time I had upset just about everybody and I was totally brassed off. I was ready to pay my fine and complete the extra forty hours and told them so. I felt I had taken away the satisfaction they would have got from saying: 'It is our decision that you will do the extra forty hours.' This way, it was my choice and I enjoyed the moment, even though they stuck me with a grand for costs.

The probation people agreed I should stop the painting and decorating and work on the move in a van so that the press couldn't get to me so easily. I worked for the local health authority delivering medical supplies and equipment – beds, mattresses, commodes, hoists for old and disabled people. Usually there were three or four

171 · Moving On

of us in a team and some of it was fairly heavy graft. We also delivered furniture on behalf of the social services to a warehouse where people such as single mothers could buy it, and then we redelivered it. There were a lot of rules and regulations laid down for community service, such as a strict ten-minute tea break, but if you were a good lad and worked hard it was so much more relaxed, and in fact I really enjoyed it.

Despite the goodwill that builds up among groups of blokes in those circumstances, you do need a break and a contrast. So I was even more grateful for my involvement with charity events such as the annual SPARKS ball, where Princess Michael, royal patron of the charity, personally thanks the celebrities who help SPARKS for their valuable work.

That year, after dinner I walked through a door and Princess Michael happened to be standing there with her husband. The music was playing and I just said: 'Do you want to dance?' No fancy angle to it or anything. We got out there and had two or three dances – I can't remember the exact music, but I think it was a bit of rock 'n' roll. I wasn't conscious of dancing with royalty or feeling any sense of awe because, with me, it's a case of what you see is what you get. I'd only have let myself down if I'd tried to put on any airs and graces. When people meet me they seem to like me for what I am, not for something or someone I'm trying to be. We didn't talk a lot because we were dancing. And anyway, the music was playing full blast.

She thanked me very much and I thanked her and took her back to her husband, and then I went and danced with Tanya. Next morning I was back on the van – probably shifting commodes.

Being made a patron of SPARKS has given me the biggest thrill of all my charity work. There is my name alongside stars such as Jimmy Tarbuck, Jimmy Hill, Henry Cooper, Sean Connery. It's an example of being wanted in the nicest possible way.

For five years or more, on Christmas morning Steve and I took toys to Hemel Hempstead Hospital and distributed them among the kids. We bought board games, Disney products, cuddly toys – a cross-section of gifts for the various age groups. It was a privilege to be able to spread a little magic every Christmas: there was something special about the faces of children in hospital that day.

Some of my fondest memories are from that short time at Leeds, where I helped raise a substantial amount of money for the local kids' home. Trouble was, the kids used to run away and head for my house. There were many occasions when I had to phone up and return them – though not before giving them a bloody good meal.

Every time I ran out on match days at Elland Road the first thing I did was to go and talk to a large group of disabled people in wheelchairs. For me to go and spend two or three minutes of my time with them was no hardship and maybe players generally might bear that in mind. It lightens the hearts of those people and suddenly their life doesn't seem too bad for a little while. When I left Leeds the disabled members of the supporters' club all chipped in and bought me a lovely painting of a countryside shooting scene. It is among the possessions I treasure most.

Fame, such as it is, has its irritating aspects if you happen to be in the wrong place at the wrong time, but I wouldn't be without it. How else would I have landed my own TV chat show? One of the Sky channels gave me a slot on their *Men and Motors* show, going out interviewing virtually whoever I liked. I had the bright idea of interviewing Mike Tyson at his home in America, and although you might think I was off my head there was a stage when a chat with Mike looked on. But instead, Steve suggested I went to see Charlton Heston.

'I can't interview Charlton Heston,' I said.

'Course you can.'

'Right, let's have a go, then. Let's do it.'

A meeting was arranged at the Dorchester Hotel. He was over here for a film premiere and it was made clear to me and the TV crew that we'd get no longer than three or four minutes. But he gave us fifteen, and later a lady from his party came to me and said: 'Charlton would like me to tell you how much he enjoyed that.' Was I made up or what? Others followed: Damon Hill, Mickey Duff and a great laugh with Peter Stringfellow at his club.

The idea expanded. We wanted a football chat show but the budget was hopeless, so the thought occurred: 'It's Men and Motors, so why don't we give them what they want – a blokey item filmed in pubs, just as if we're sitting chatting with the boys?' So that's what we did, talking to the likes of Terry Neil, the former Arsenal manager, and referee David Elleray. Successful? I was only voted New Presenter of the Year at the Sky awards, that's all!

Chapter 22

Goodbye Football, Hello Hollywood

And then came a part in a film. A proper film. The part of the tough-guy debt-collector, Big Chris, in Lock, Stock and Two Smoking Barrels. It all began with a phone call from Guy Ritchie, who wrote and directed it, and Matthew Vaughn, the producer. Apparently, the notes about Big Chris had described the character as 'very cool. An aura about him. Respected, but you wouldn't want to cross this man. If he loses it, he loses it. Similar to Vinnie Jones the footballer.'

I'd once had a walk-on part in the TV programme Ellington, which Matthew and Guy had seen. So when they were casting the film, Matthew suggested: 'If Chris is like Vinnie Jones, why don't we ask Vinnie Jones to play him?' After a meeting at Stoke Poges Golf Club, the next hurdle was a screen test for the woman said to have discovered Arnold Schwarzenegger. Guy told me: 'The part's yours, but you'll need to get past her first.' Panic! I began by doing the part in keeping with the script I'd memorised, but she said: 'It's okay, it's pretty good, but now play it as yourself. Not as Big Chris. Do it as Vinnie Jones.' So I did just that and they were over the moon.

The film was hard work, really hard. I would train in the mornings and go straight to the film set in the afternoons. Shortage of

As Big Chris in Lock, Stock and Two Smoking Barrels. Little Chris was played by Peter McNicholl.

money meant it had to be shot from week to week. I remember once having the weekend off because there wasn't enough in the kitty to film on the Saturday. There were many times when we thought it had all gone down the pan. We all owe a lot to Trudie Styler, Sting's wife and one of the executive producers, who kept it afloat. She kept telling people what a good movie it was, and her support for it persuaded people to help with the finance. I think she and Sting put money in as well.

Personally, much as I relished it all, I had no illusions of film-star status. I had loved my TV chat show – it had been a bit of fun on the side, something else to do, and kept me out of the pub. Filming was refreshing as well, enjoyable work alongside good people. Even though, once people found out I was doing it, I had the piss taken out of me mercilessly. 'Here comes the movie star,' that kind of thing. You know how footballers can be.

But that film part changed the direction of my life. It had been quite a journey – from juvenile petty thief, washer-up of pots and pans with his life in a plastic bin-liner and hod-carrier on building

A scene from Lock, Stock and Two Smoking Barrels.

sites to fourteen years as a professional footballer, captaining Wales, playing at Wembley and gaining an FA Cup-winner's medal – with no end of dog's abuse and resentment along the way. And now I was soon to have a home address, however temporary, in Beverly Hills. If somebody had made it up, nobody would have believed it.

I could never have guessed what would happen once the film was released. It was just something I was invited to do, something that appealed, and I never gave it much more thought than that. Until I saw the movie at the wrap party, the celebration at the end of filming for all those involved, from the cast and directors to the tea girls and truck drivers. When I saw myself up there on the big screen a powerful sensation hit me right in the stomach. It felt as if I had just swallowed ten jars of butterflies. But, my God, I felt so proud by the time the credits rolled. Even then, despite the satisfaction of believing I had done a decent job for a first-time effort, it never occurred to me that I might have something of a future in this game rather than the one where we booted a ball around.

It wasn't until the London premiere that any such thoughts entered my head. Dustin Hoffman was among the big names present, and as I had my picture taken with him he called me something like 'the new Bruce Willis'. Perhaps he was just being kind, but as we chatted I turned round and saw my dad with tears of pride streaming down his face.

The old floodgates had opened again.

Tanya's emotions showed themselves in a different way. She just kept giggling. What was nice, too, after receiving so much criticism and ridicule as a footballer, was picking up the papers and reading: 'Vinnie Jones' contribution to the movie was impressive.'

Everybody congratulated me. All the old pals from Bedmond and around, those from the Under-18 football team, all of them said: 'Well done, Jonah, 'cos we remember where you came from.' And so do I. My mates are still my mates and always will be. When the success of *Lock, Stock* hit the headlines, I looked through the window one morning at the builders working outside our new house. I looked at Paul Hobbs, who had been with me way back in the Watford boys' team, and I thought: 'Yeah, Paul looks as happy as a king as well. He's gone on to be a great brickie.' No difference, really. Different jobs, but we still look on each other in the same way.

Guy and Matthew had always said that if we got back the million quid the film cost to make it would have been a success. A million quid? It took nearly £14 million at the box office alone, and the videos made many millions more. Unbelievable. Oh yes, and there was the small matter of me winning a Best Newcomer award, Best Debut and about four or five others. I remember saying to Guy: 'This could become serious, couldn't it?'

He replied: 'Vin, I'd forget all about football if I were you. I think you are on your way.'

The American premiere of Lock, Stock enabled me to meet influential people, casting agents at Paramount and Warner. I started to think that this was going to be my living now, because everybody was saying how good I was and a couple of new scripts arrived. I was flown all over the place, first class; there were limousines here, there and everywhere; private jets to Vegas and back for lunch. I was winning more awards – The Empire Variety Club of Great Britain, the Odeon Cinemas' award. I was invited to all the functions and making friends with people like Michael Caine, Bob Hoskins, all the big hitters. And I was accepted by them. Suddenly, it was as if the top movie stars, like Kate Winslet, were my new pals. Remember how I used to run when I wasn't wanted? Well, I found myself in another gang now, and felt at home and comfortable. But there was still a bit of caution there. I kept thinking to myself: 'This is all right, but am I on an escalator going up or an escalator going down?' And you can only be on an escalator moving in any direction for so long. Once you are at the top, if you don't step forward, you fall over.

In the United States, the marketing wasn't done very well, so the film didn't take the cinemas by storm. But word got round eventually, and video sales went through the roof. In the end, the film earned, I believe, somewhere around $15 million. So yes, my earnings from the film were substantial, though nowhere near as high as some might have you believe. They were paid in stages, but I left mine in the pot so that eventually there would be one handy cheque and it could all go to Harefield Hospital. If you buy something from a traveller he usually gives you a few quid back – money for luck, they call it. And I've always been a believer in luck money.

There is no way I can repay the people at Harefield for the help they have given and still provide for Tanya. It incenses both of us to think that the hospital is under threat. The dedication of all those who work at that place is phenomenal. All I can do is make little gestures to show my personal gratitude.

As the big film studio doors began to open for me, the dressing-room door was about to close. Vinnie Jones, football manager, was not to be. Not at QPR, at any rate.

On a Saturday towards the end of September 1998, we played at Oxford. I had been sent off playing for the reserves against Swindon a week or two earlier – an off-the-ball incident, according to the referee, but much ado about not a lot, if you ask me. Although I wanted to play at Oxford, Ray Harford decided against it, leaving the midfield intact and saying, 'Let them get on with it.' Oxford got on with it a lot better than QPR and beat us easily.

It was the last time I saw the lads.

I went berserk with them in the dressing-room because they had shown absolutely no will to win. That kind of attitude was completely unacceptable to me, and I blew my top. Fourteen years in the pro game, and suddenly, within four months of joining QPR, I was already disillusioned.

When we stopped at Wycombe on the way home for Ray to collect his car, his rotten day was completed by the discovery that somebody had broken into it and nicked the stereo. 'What else can happen?' he wondered wearily. As he drove off, I thought to myself: 'This bloke can't take any more.'

The next day Nick Blackburn, right-hand man to chairman Chris Wright, told me over the phone that Ray had resigned. Then he went on: 'We're putting Iain Dowie in charge. We've had a meeting, and because of your commitments and one thing and another, we've made him manager for the time being.' I was astounded and angry. Dowie, the number three, had been promoted over my head. My understanding had been that when Ray left the club, I, as his number two, would be first to be considered for the job of manager.

I was thirty-four years old and bursting to have a go at management – my way. I met Chris Wright and the other officials on the Monday, and it remains my biggest regret, even now, that they didn't give me the chance, despite my pleas and assurances that I would commit myself completely to the job. Instead they booted me right in the teeth. Although Dowie's appointment was temporary, and they invited me to apply for the manager's job as advertised, I was having none of it. It became clear they couldn't afford to pay up the two and a half years of my contract and it seemed they didn't even want me to play. They asked for 'time to think about it'. In the meantime, I received a phone call from the United States.

It came around ten o'clock on a Monday evening, and it was from my agent from the States (you have to have one, don't you?), Nick Styne. His company looks after people like Cameron Diaz, Sir Anthony Hopkins and Jimmy Nail, and I was fortunate that they took me on. Nick told me that Jerry Bruckheimer, the man who produced The Rock and Top Gun, had been on 'and would like to meet you, Wednesday'. Hollywood? By three o'clock on Wednesday?

'How do I manage that?'

'There's a first-class return ticket

waiting for you at the airport for the noon flight tomorrow.'

First-class return flight? I'd have bloody well swum the Atlantic for the chance of a part in a blockbuster, but I didn't want to show how keen I was. Not before I'd heard what they had to say.

By this time, Peter Burrell had taken over as my UK agent, Steve now having his hands full with a computer company in which we'd invested. Peter has represented top jockey Frankie Dettori since Frankie was sixteen and has done a fantastic job for him. Peter is the nicest bloke, and very imaginative – and I'm not just saying that because of the lucrative deals he's done for me. When I discussed the invitation to America with him, he assured me: 'If they weren't ninety-nine per cent certain you're what they're looking for, they wouldn't send you a first-class return ticket.'

As luck would have it, Tanya was in the States at the time – I'd arranged for her to visit Graceland for her birthday – but was flying home as I headed out. She was so excited – we both were – and with all the uncertainty about my future, I needed that part. I had been sent the script, for a $100 million production called Gone in Sixty Seconds, two or three weeks earlier. I'd read it several times already but spent three hours going over it again at the Sheraton Hotel in Santa Monica on the Wednesday morning. The part they had in mind for me, the Sphinx, didn't involve a lot of dialogue. It is all in the strength of the character until, at the end, the Sphinx makes a big speech that stuns everybody.

A limo took me to Bruckheimer's office, an ordinary place from the outside, but massively impressive inside. As I waited I sat there peering at all the credits around the place, the honours, the discs for the film soundtracks. Then I was introduced to Bruckheimer, the director, and Chad Omen, his right-hand man. They were sitting behind the biggest desk I had ever seen. It must have been twenty feet long. This was no casting: they were simply asking me how much I enjoyed doing Lock, Stock, how many takes I'd needed and other general questions. I sensed that Dominic Sena, the director, was quite excited, especially when Jerry just looked across at him and asked: 'Well, do you want me to hire him?'

'Yeah, yeah, get him on board.'

'Welcome aboard,' Jerry said to me.

Just like that. The chat, the questions, the decision, the whole thing took no more than half an hour.

'Thanks a lot, Vinnie. We'll be in touch,' they said. 'We'll talk to your agent. He'll send your lawyers in during the next few days and we'll do the deal. A house will be sorted out for you here in Beverly Hills or wherever you want it. Just come out and have a look around.'

Back at the airport I phoned everyone and their aunt from the first-class lounge. On the plane, even though I was absolutely knackered, I felt like running up and down the gangways telling everybody who was prepared to listen. Then the fear hit me. Not only had the contracts not been signed, but I suddenly realised I hadn't even asked them what the money was! I hadn't given a thought to what the film might earn me, although I did know the star, Nicolas Cage, was said to be getting $20 million. Me? It might be a couple of million, I said to myself. Maybe $1 million? Well, half a million at worst. I spent eleven hours in the air with all this whirring round in my head and not a minute's kip.

The QPR situation had to be brought to a head. Gerry Francis, who had done so well for them in the early nineties, was reappointed and quite rightly explained to me that he was bringing in his own number two. At least he put his cards on the table. I felt QPR were trying to force me out by getting me to train with the kids. In the end I made a decision. I told them I would walk away if they paid me up to the end of the season, letting them off with two years of my money, and that's how it was resolved.

It was done in the nick of time, because the very next day they read in the newspapers that I was on my way to America. I enjoyed the feeling that I had called their bluff. But at the beginning of the week it had looked as if my entire American dream might be wrecked.

Peter had called. 'Major panic. You have to be at a meeting at the American Embassy.' The conviction for ABH and that dispute with the neighbour in Redbourn had come back to haunt me and there was a real danger that I wouldn't get a work permit for the States. I was swamped by dark thoughts. 'That's it. I've come all this way and worked so bloody hard. A hundred million-dollar movie, and they're not going to let me in.' I was really depressed and told Tanz I knew it had all been too good to be true, the way everything had slotted into place for me so brilliantly. As ever, she looked on the bright side and insisted I was worrying too much.

Thankfully Tanya's unbelievable optimism and belief in fate was completely justified. Apparently, convictions are graded, and my one-off first offence obviously came into not too serious a category in comparison with, say, drugs or sex-offending. I was okay. I'll never forget those four beautiful words: 'Here are your documents.'

I confer with Guy Ritchie on almost everything I do, even now, and when I got my big break in the States he told me: 'Go out there and get your face known around Hollywood. This is a massive movie, Vinnie – Nicolas Cage, no less. I knew it was going to happen for you, but not this quick!'

There were some more valuable words of advice, and caution, from 'Harry' Bassett before I flew out to LA. 'Remember Sweden, Jonah. You went out and did the business. You've got to do the same again now. Don't be thinking you have to prove you are the tough guy by getting involved in bar brawls. Stay away from it all and do what they are paying you to do. This is a big chance, son.'

I had to be in Hollywood

two weeks before filming started, for wardrobe, make-up, hair-
styists, rehearsals, all that stuff. Graham Coles came with me to LA,
and we were taken to an hotel right on Sunset Strip. Colesy and
Jonesy with adjoining suites. A fair distance from Hemel and
Bedmond. Had the boys made it, or what? The first phone call I took
was from the front desk: 'Your car has been delivered, Mr Jones.' It
was a Honda, a lovely model, but I felt cheeky enough to ring up
and exchange it for a Mustang. Convertible, of course. Me and
Colesy, roof off, flying about up and down Sunset Strip. No, I can't
say I felt depressed about losing the chance to manage QPR.

I was nervous on the first day on the set. The thought of Nicolas
Cage, Angelina Jolie and the other stars – and Robert Duvall wasn't
even there yet. Somebody told me: 'Bobby's really looking forward
to meeting you. He's followed your football career, especially your
time with Chelsea.' That perked me up a bit. And when one of the
PAs said how much he had enjoyed Lock, Stock, I began to feel a part
of what was going on rather than like a spectator.

Colesy and I were taken to our trailer. There were three or four
of them the size of houses, for the stars. Nick had about four for
himself – one was his gym, another for his chef, another for himself,
the fourth for make-up. Come to think of it, he more or less had his
own little village. My trailer was ten or twelve feet long. It had a little
shower and toilet, a little front room with a telly and a settee that
could be made into a bed. But I could never get on that because
Colesy was always asleep there. It might not have been as big as the
others, but this was a trailer alongside a Hollywood film set provided for the use of Vinnie Jones. Where were they now, all those critics
who had slaughtered me down the years?

Chapter 23

The Big Speech

Colesy and I spent two weeks in our hotel while we were looking for a house. I had thought we would find somewhere for a couple of grand a month, but I realised it was going to cost slightly more when the estate agent pointed out that we were looking at properties worth $10 million or more.

Turning into one driveway, he commented: 'If you fancy this house, you'll be the second British actor in a row to live here.'

'Oh yeah, and who's the other one, then?' I asked.

'Hugh Grant.'

'Right, I'll have it!' I turned to Colesy. 'We've got five or six months out here. If we never come back, at least we'll have some great memories. We'll do it properly.' At a proper price as well – $11,500 a month, furnished. The house was owned by an Italian. When you first drove up, through the electric gates, the place was white and square and didn't look out of the ordinary. We pulled up in the carport. This wasn't the main house at all: it turned out to be the maid's quarters.

There were beautiful trees everywhere and archways of roses leading to the main door of the house, a lovely, massive white door.

When you opened it… wow! Marble everywhere, glorious paintings and, Jesus, take a look at that staircase. Marble again, like all the floors. A magnificent, grand, sweeping staircase straight out of one of those American musicals. Four double bedrooms, all en-suite, all with french windows opening on to a patio. We walked along a vast corridor, beautifully furnished with little tables, paintings, candlesticks – all sumptuous. The kitchen was to the right, and then a huge dining-room with a twelve-seater table. We walked into the even larger lounge.

'Press this button,' the agent told me.

I pressed and a television appeared. I pressed another and the music system burst into life. There was a bar with a fridge, great big sliding patio doors and there it was – just three feet away, a swimming pool to die for. We were to take a few risks in the weeks to come, jumping off the living-room roof straight in to the water.

The house was built on a hillside from where we had a panoramic view of everything. Marla Maples' place was a little below it. It was such a glorious setting, and so tranquil. At night we would look across and see all the lights against the darkness of the hillside. It was as if we were seeing thousands of fireflies. Awesome.

The whole top floor of the house was our suite. It must have been sixty feet long. I couldn't wait for Tanya to see all this. The bathroom was vast, with a huge sunken marble bath, and I've never seen a bigger bed or walk-in wardrobe. Another room was laid out as a private office. There was no other word for it: this stage of Vinnie Jones's life had turned into a fairytale.

I phoned all my old mates and told them: 'You've got to get out here. You've got to come and see this. You won't believe what's happened to me.' We lost count of the number of times Colesy drove to the airport and back to pick up my family and Tanya's and all the friends who came to visit. He must have made the trip on sixty occasions at least. Because I only had the one big piece of dialogue to deliver, there weren't many lines for me to learn, so basically I took the whole of Hertfordshire on holiday. It would be golf just about every day and back to that gorgeous house. And the nice feeling increased when I heard that the media at home were backing me.

When my mates arrived and saw our surroundings, they either

laughed or screamed their heads off, yelling: 'You've cracked it, Jonah, boy.' It was a perfect lifestyle for Tanya, because she had no stress at all. All she had to do was take a towel to the poolside, stretch out and relax. For a meal with the kids we'd order pizza or something. Out there you can dial-a-pizza, dial-a-table, dial-a-phone, dial-an-extra-bed.

'Is that Mr Jones?'

'Yeah. Three more beds? Bring 'em up.'

My sister, the kids, Tanya's mate Mandy, my mum, Tanya's mum, Maureen – there were five or six of them sharing one room. It was like a barracks. Tanya became the tour operator, pointing out the sights: Hollywood, the stars, the celebrity handprints, the beach. At one time there were seventeen of us in the house for dinner. We lived a lot on salads and fresh fish. Sometimes the girls would do it, and we were grateful for Colesy's liking for cooking, too – he did a mean barbecue.

I had to perform on the first day of filming, so there wasn't much time to worry about it beforehand. It was the scene at the Ferrari warehouse. I couldn't make conversation with the other actors, the names I'd only ever read about; in fact I froze. They were totally relaxed and telling jokes, but I didn't even understand their humour. They weren't sure about me, either, this strange English footballer, and must have been wondering who the hell I was. So I just did my own thing at first.

I was like a spare wotsit at a wedding. 'Here you go again, Jonesy, boy,' I said to myself. 'You're out of your depth, son. Bitten off more than you can chew this time.' I felt a bit of an imposter. The big names around me had all done some twenty films and I'd done one – and a film none of them had seen or even heard of, at that. I started playing mind games with myself, worrying that Lock, Stock had been a one-off. After all, I'd had Guy Ritchie and Matthew Vaughn to lean on then. If I didn't get it right this time, would they sack me? Was Nicolas Cage thinking he was working with an amateur? My arse was going like the clappers. I had to produce. But could I? Panic!

Colesy was great, because he watched it all on the monitor with the director. He gave me terrific moral support. He was always on the set, he was with me every day for six months. I wouldn't have legged it without him because I'm not one to run away, but I don't

think I would have been as good as I became if he hadn't been there. He told me he'd been earwigging and heard the director say that Vinnie was awesome, and that they were so pleased with me. He was earwigging all over the place. He was rock solid for me.

During the first week, Nicolas pulled me to one side and said: 'I'm having a party. The chef's going to make some pizza. Why don't you come up to the house?' I began to feel more a part of it then.

We didn't make Nicolas's party in the end, so the first one we went to was Angelina Jolie's birthday party. 'I'm not inviting everybody,' she told Colesy and me, 'but do come up.' It was smashing, but nothing like the parties we were used to at home. They finish out there at around eleven o'clock at night because filming tends to run from dawn till dusk, though a lot of our movie was done at night. They're not boozy parties, either. You don't see people falling about or in any way the worse for drink. It's all very sensible. Angelina made a big fuss of us, though.

The reason why my character, the Sphinx, doesn't speak throughout the film is because he has been traumatised. It's not clear whether he can't talk or just refuses to. But as we filmed all the action stuff, I knew there was a big moment waiting for me: the moment when the Sphinx speaks at last. The big speech, the climax of the film. The trouble was, I had no idea when it would come. Scenes were shot according to location, so we would jump from one part of the script to another and I was always expecting the call:

'This is it, Vinnie.'

I was careful not to irritate people. Nick and I filmed together quite a lot, but between scenes I never knew whether to start a conversation, crack a joke, or what on earth to do. I didn't want to risk driving him mad if he was memorising his lines, so I just sat there in silence. We got on great, but there were times when I would try to avoid him. I felt a bit like a kid standing outside the dressing-rooms waiting for a footballer's autograph. I'd been signing them for fifteen years, but now I was the child with the book and the pencil. It wasn't that I was starstruck, just that I wanted to do the right thing. But there was no one to tell me what it was. While everyone else stood around talking about this film or that, I felt like an alien from outer space. Which in a way I was, coming from the world of football, which none of them knew anything about.

In the end we got to the final week of filming, some six months on, before I got my call. By then there had been an enormous build-up, and I sensed that everybody was looking forward to it, even Nick and Angelina. The prospect gave me a tremendous buzz, though I wasn't nervous because I had become more confident as time had gone on. But how was I to know that when my big day arrived the entire cast would be sitting there? Nick Cage, Angelina, Bobby Duvall – all of them. Confidence in front of the camera and enjoying the company of your colleagues round a barbecue is one thing. Knowing that they're going to be watching you during one of the greatest challenges of your career is quite another.

Everyone was shouting and cheering – all these superstar actors, all the assistants, camera crew, make-up artists, sound and lighting people. Everything was ready and everybody was waiting for me to say my piece. I looked around. That's when I started to tremble. I was suddenly aware of my trouser legs. I could feel them rubbing slightly as my legs shook inside them. You could touch the tension.

My cue was two lads in discussion and the words: 'I wish I was Toby, man.' I could feel my heart thumping. I had been learning my lines for the previous six months, anticipating the moment when I would launch into my speech: 'If his premature demise has in some way enlightened the rest of you as to the grim finish below the glossy veneer of criminal life…' Yeah, I know it off by heart, it's sure to be okay, Vinnie.

And then the director came up to me and said: 'Oh, sorry, I forgot to tell you. We've had to change it. We haven't killed Toby, so where you say, "If his premature demise has in some way," we now want you to say, "If his unpleasant wounding has in some way".'

'Hold on a minute! You can't be telling me at this stage!' But they were, and you have no option. I was trying to grasp it: 'If his… If his… If his unpleasant wounding has in some way…'

Two words altered. Two bloody words, that's all, but you've no idea what a difference it made. And then they said more changes were needed later in the speech. Six months working up to this, and then, half an hour from the call for action and, in front of Nick and Angelina and Bobby and everybody, I'm told the goalposts have moved. I'm pitched into sheer blind panic. I know I haven't got it in the bag.

But this is it. My head is spinning, I'm sweating profusely, the

Left: With mates
Frankie Dettori,
Dennis Wise and
Ronnie Wood at the
London premiere of
Gone in Sixty Seconds.

Right: Arriving with
Tanya at the London
premiere of Gone in
Sixty Seconds.

Splashing around in
the pool with Kaley in
Beverly Hills on
Christmas Day, 2000.

trouser legs are going again. And the heart. Bump, bump, bump.

'I wish I was Toby, man.'

Here goes. I kept thinking, 'Unpleasant wounding, unpleasant wounding.' I had to lean forwards as I said my bit and pick up a bottle of beer. I couldn't let them see that I was shaking like a leaf, but I couldn't do anything to stop it. I leaned forwards: 'If his unpleasant wounding…' I thought: 'Where is this other different line? Please?'

The other actors in the scene looked astonished. They were supposed to: they were amazed that the Sphinx had spoken at last. But I was struck by a sudden paranoia that they were horrified at me. A thousand things rushed into my mind at once and I just went blank. Completely bleedin' blank. I looked around in desperation. I was one millimetre away from making a run for it, away from this total humiliation. I could not see the next line, or even the next word, to save my life. The pause just went on and on and on. Jesus, I can feel the panic all over again as I recall those seconds.

There was only one thing for me to do.

'I'm sorry.'

'Don't worry about it,' Nick Cage said. 'Just don't worry about it.'

It was more than the shakes now. Vinnie Jones had turned into a complete jelly.

'Don't worry,' the call went up. 'We'll go again.'

That wasn't what my head was saying to me. 'Fuck going again,' I thought. 'I don't want to go again if I get it wrong a second time. I'll be finished.'

I grabbed my script with the new lines. I read it and read it and read it again. 'That's it. That's the other bloody line.'

'His death carries with it an inherent mobility' had changed to 'His injuries carry with them…' I went through it again. It was basically just one poxy word, but for me it felt like life or death. I looked up and saw Colesy signalling his encouragement.

And I did it. I bloody did it. I delivered the lines. But at the end of my speech I had to pick up the bottle of beer and have a swig, and after Nicolas Cage said: 'Hey, man, thought you was from Long Beach,' I had to put it down again. I was shaking so much that if it had been a cup of tea I'd have scattered its contents all over the set.

That was the master take. You then have to do the close-ups, so you actually do the speech about twenty times more, but once you know you've got the master in the bag, there's no problem.

Robert Duvall was very kind and understanding. He told me later: 'I've sometimes needed ten goes at one word, Vinnie. It's a mental block, that's all. It happens to the best actors in the world. Usually a good director will see you're having trouble and scrap it for a while. It happens to Travolta, but he can say, "That's it, finished, can't do it. I'm tired. Come back tomorrow."'

But I'd done it, and everybody was telling me that I was 'awesome' and encouraging me to 'keep doing what you're doing'. In football I'd always been the one doing the encouraging and cajoling; now it was me wanting and needing to be led. I think they appreciated me more for that. It goes a long way when you ask if you are doing things right, or how to do them better. You don't deserve the benefit of other people's experience if you come across as a smartarse who thinks he knows it all.

That big scene of mine always gets a laugh. It's funny for me to sit in a cinema and see the reaction of the audience. Little can they have known, until now, the nightmare I went through to pull it off.

There were some lovely, fun times during the making of Gone in Sixty Seconds. I became really close to Bobby Duvall. He and Nick Cage are completely different. Nick is more the shy guy who keeps himself to himself, though we did talk quite a lot about our kids – his boy is the same age as Aaron. Bobby wanted me in Up for the Cup, the movie he did with Ali MacGraw. Having just come out of football, I thought I'd be laying myself open to a hammering from the critics. Mind you, in spare moments, I did get the lads playing football in the parking lot. Most of them joined in, with Bobby cheering us on and Nick Cage coming to watch. It was then that I really relaxed and wondered why I'd got myself into such a state early on. They loved me out there, no bull, and they all genuinely wanted me to do well.

Off the set, it was usually just Colesy and me. We really didn't know anyone else. You often get people saying 'Give me a ring, we'll play some golf, we'll go and have lunch,' but it never happens. We did become quite matey with Steve Jones, who used to be with the Sex Pistols and who lived close by. He's settled for a quieter existence now and is deeply involved with Alcoholics Anonymous. We went to a couple of places with Steve, though he doesn't really like going out much.

I just thoroughly relished what I now call 'the moment': my first experience of working life as a film actor in the United States. LA has a terrific quality of life, too – I'm certain the beautiful climate plays a part in making everyone so cheerful. You get up in the morning, brush the teeth, have a shower, put the shorts and trainers on and get out there. The people are so friendly. There is none of the anger that seems to infect life in Britain. I think much of that problem is down to the stress of everyday living: the hours, the difficulty of simply getting about the place. Coming home and experiencing the frustration on the roads crammed into this small country of ours makes you realise what a disgrace they are. It's no wonder they generate so much ill feeling. In the States, parents spend so much of their time enjoying their children. What can you do with the kids over here when it rains so much? I think of Guy Ritchie and his wife, Madonna, cooking on their barbecue every night of the week. We can't compare life in Britain with life in a sunny place, can we?

I finished my last bit of filming and at the end of it somebody announced: 'Ladies and gentlemen, Vinnie is wrapped.' Then the make-up girls and wardrobe people brought out a cake, opened the champagne and little presents were handed around. You say good-bye to everybody and suddenly it dawns that this is it, it's finished. I didn't want it to end. I didn't want to be packing our things and putting them in the car and heading for the airport, leaving behind that wonderful house with its full-time maid and the gardener and pool-man who arrived twice a week.

As I flew home alone, leaving Colesy to close up the house, I reflected on it all. I felt I'd flown the flag and done well. I started to feel chuffed, too. It was a bit like returning from Sweden all those years back, when I'd gone out as a boy and come back a man. And, in a sense, the same thing was happening again. My start in football and my start in the movie business had been very similar. Staring out of the window as we landed at Heathrow, I thought: 'It's nice to be back, but I could turn round and fly to America again tomorrow.' I really wanted to do another movie out there. I suppose I was hoping this could be the start of something big. In the meantime, I had another film to do in England.

I had great fun making *Gone in Sixty Seconds* and enjoyed meeting up with fellow actors like Angelina Jolie at the premiere.

Within about a week of my return from the States we started
filming *Snatch*, a second Guy Ritchie film, which had been lined up
while I was away. I'd learned the script already. At first it was intended that I would play two parts – twin brothers, but changes had been
made to the original idea and Guy had rewritten the script. He told
me: 'I've got some good news and some bad news. The good news
is that Brad Pitt wants to be in the movie.'

'And the bad news? Am I still in the film?'

'Of course you are. But I'm moving away from the idea of the
twins. I'm giving Brad his own character with the gypsies, and I see
you as Bullet-Tooth Tony, this guy who knows London and all the
villains.'

I was a bit worried at first because the character struck me as an
extension of Big Chris, and I feared people would think I was playing the same role over again. But Guy assured me: 'This geezer's
completely different.' I had one key scene, where I sit talking to
three black guys who have guns pointed at me. Guy insisted: 'If you
get that right, you can steal the movie.'

I know I was lucky. I'd already worked in the company of some

With Guy Ritchie and
Jason Statham who
starred with me in
Snatch.

massive names in the film world: Robert Duvall, Nicolas Cage, Angelina Jolie, and now Brad Pitt. And John Travolta was to come. And every film I've made has reached number one in this country. I've set good standards, so I know that each step I take from now on has to be carefully considered. And, yes, I've made my million!

But it's not quite the money people might imagine. Out of your fee you have to pay lawyers, accountants, agents, a manager – and tax, of course. You end up banking about a third of the gross figure.

Snatch came at a good time for me because I had been to America, crapped myself, recovered and arrived home confident. Before shooting started Guy said to me: 'There are a couple of actors who are first-timers, so I want you to give them your support where you can.' Suddenly I was made to feel like the captain again. During rehearsals, I remember, I was able to deliver my two main speeches straight off the top of my head. The other boys, who'd had weeks and weeks to learn their lines, were struggling and had to keep referring to the script – just like me in Hollywood.

Snatch took about three months to film and we were all delighted with it. Our confidence was confirmed by reactions at the British premiere. But nothing prepared me for what happened at the Hollywood premiere: after my main scene, everybody stood up and applauded! My American agent, Nick Styne, was sitting next to me. 'Have you any idea just how awesome that is?' he said. That audience included people like Madonna, Dustin Hoffman, Gwyneth Paltrow, Quentin Tarantino – it was like a Who's Who of Hollywood. It was like winning the Cup final – your moment, you're the man, and nobody can imagine the scale of your joy. When you have somebody like Tarantino coming up to you, not just to say hello but to congratulate you – 'Vinnie, that was brilliant. That scene, man, terrific' – and Dustin Hoffman insisting on shaking your hand, you know you've done well because, if you hadn't, they wouldn't want to know.

They staged the party afterwards at a big nightclub with a huge marquee out at the back. Everybody in town wanted to be there, and it was absolutely heaving. It developed into a double party because Madonna and Guy had a separate one of their own. About eighty people continued the celebration at their place. I'd flown out two of my old mates, Cal Jenkins and Seamus Byrne, who'd thought it was a wind-up until they received their flight tickets. I put them up

A scene from Snatch.

at the Four Seasons hotel with us. For me it was like taking two younger brothers on a guided tour of Charlie's Chocolate Factory. Seamus kept laughing all the time and introducing himself to everybody, saying: 'Hello, I'm Vinnie's friend…' Then he'd walk across to Cal: 'Hey, can you believe this is happening?'

They left for home the day before we did and their eyes filled up when they thanked me. 'We just can't put it into words, but this is the biggest thing that has ever happened to us.' It was great to be able to show them that side of my life.

While I was in America for the premiere of Sixty Seconds, I thought I'd cracked it for another film. Nick Styne had suggested I stayed around for another couple of weeks to meet a couple of casting directors and see what was going. Within days I was in touching distance of a part in a movie called Gangs of New York with Cameron Diaz and Brad Pitt. I went through the lines – it was an Irish character, and I've got quite a good Irish accent, because of Tanya's side of the family – and I was so excited when I was told they were over the moon with the way I'd done it. But back over the Atlantic in Hertfordshire, the waiting went on and on. I'd returned to America with Tanya and repeated my screen test by the time the call came: 'Sorry, buddy, you haven't got it.' They explained that they'd decided to cast the character in the fifty to fifty-five age bracket. It was my first knock-back.

That was at eleven o'clock one morning. At twelve, the phone rang again. It was Nick. 'What time can you be down at Universal Studios?'

'Why, what's up?'

'Travolta's doing this movie called Swordfish. You've got to go down and meet one of the executive producers. And phone Dominic Sena first. He's directing it.'

'What's the crack, Dom?'

'I'm doing this movie with Travolta. Mercenaries and stuff. You'll be brilliant for it. And you can speak with an English accent, because there'll be Russians, Japanese, English, Chinese and Americans. It's a good role – Marco – and all your scenes are with Travolta. But we've two concerns.'

'And they are?'

'One is your accent in Lock, Stock.'

I had to explain that my accent had been exaggerated because we were supposed to be from the East End of London. 'That's the way they talk. It's called Cockney.'

'Great, fine,' Dom said. 'Just speak as properly as you can. And the second thing is that we need to see you in a suit. You'd be wearing a suit all the time in this film, but the people have only seen you in Lock, Stock.'

A suit they wanted, so a suit they'd get – and do I look sharp with a suit on. I only put on the cream number, don't I. Drive down there in the Cadi, roof off. Remember the old days, when the big stars drove into the studios big style? That was me. I glided in saying to myself: 'I'm a film star – and not Mickey Mouse.' I was hoping they could see me from the window. I was invited into the office of Jonathan Crane, the executive producer: 'Come in, Vinnie. Come in. Thought you were great in Lock, Stock—' And then the bloody phone rang, and he must have been talking on it for twenty minutes.

This was my big interview, and I was just left sitting there thinking: 'This ain't going too well at all. Maybe I should go home.'

But there was no hanging round once Jonathan put the phone down: 'Right, Vinnie. Sorry. John Travolta saw Lock, Stock last night. Loves you. You're in. Marco.' Just like that.

'The other thing was, I wanted to see you dressed differently from in Lock, Stock, but…' And he waved his hand in approval of the suit and said: 'Fantastic.' Dominic had done me a real favour by marking my card. Back behind the wheel of the Cadi, the reality struck me. I'd landed the part on the word of John Travolta, one of the best actors in the world. Not a lot of people can say that. I got on the mobile to Nick. 'Did you ask him how much?' he asked.

'Oh no! I've gone and done it again!' I'd completely forgotten to check. I'd been so chuffed that money hadn't entered my head. But the parties got together and I think the initial offer was doubled. Allowance thrown in, plus four first-class Virgin flights for the family. And this time a forty-foot trailer!

Once I started work, in September 2000, I got to know the studio driver who picked me up to take me in every day. Buck Holland was in the movie The Wild Bunch and he knew all the tricks of the trade. We became really pally. 'You're on your way up,' he said to me one morning. 'Why? Because this is your second film out here, and you've got the star trailer.'

'Is that such a big deal?'

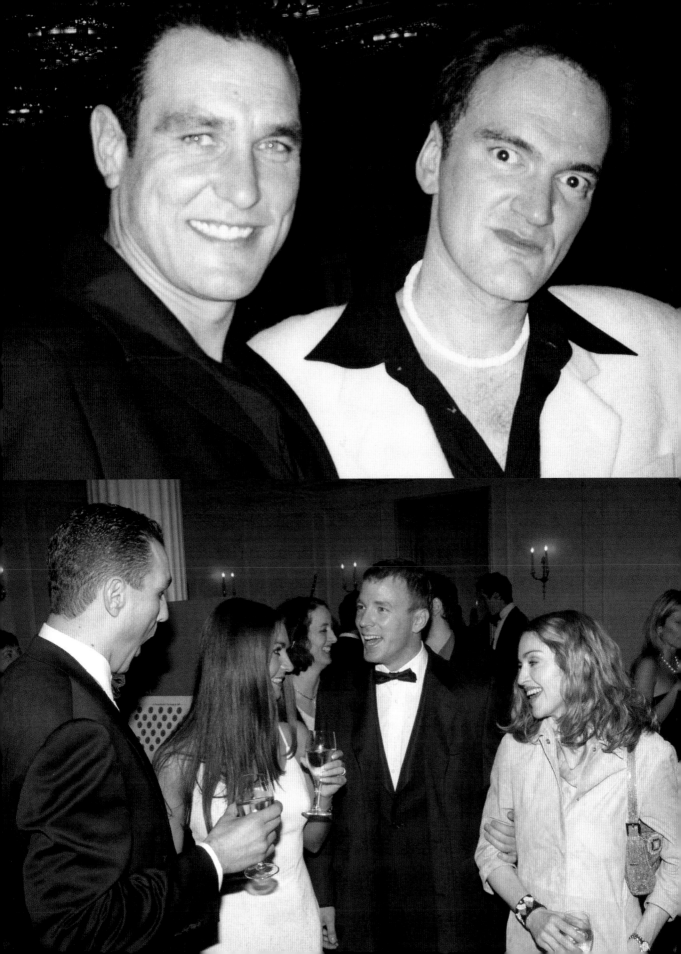

'You're in Hollywood, man. The bigger the trailer, the more important you are. Second movie! You've got some powerful people behind you.'

So, another day, another dollar. Another movie, this time a $100 million movie – and, yes, another wonderful house to live in. Tanya and I must have looked at a hundred. I had a twelve-grand-a-month allowance and we were viewing six- to seven-grand-a-month places. We both knew they simply weren't big enough. Even though we'd been there and done it, lived in a swish pad big enough to entertain the whole of Hertfordshire, Tanya looked at me and smiled: 'Once more.'

The agent knew, the moment I phoned. 'Yeah,' I said, 'we want something bigger. Four or five bedrooms, swimming pool, tennis court, the whole works.' He knew just the place. As we were looking round this magnificent house, set in about four acres, with volleyball court and floodlit tennis court, this elderly black fella came up. 'Go ahead, carry on,' he said.

'Excuse me, do you work here?'

we asked.

'Work here? Shit, man, this is my house. Bill Withers – nice to meet you. Have you seen everything you want?'

We took the house. Never mind my allowance of twelve grand a month. I was happy to pay the fourteen grand. And that was unfurnished. It cost me another fifteen hundred a month to rent all the furniture. We hired everything, down to the eggcups. A couple of days after we moved in, Bill called round with a gift: some cushions for the sunbeds round the pool. What a nice touch. What a lovely fella. We talked quite a lot because he often popped round. You'd look out of the window of a morning and he'd be out there cleaning the pool.

We were soon back into the American way of life – in fact we spent Christmas and New Year in Las Vegas. What a place! At one stage we found ourselves sitting less than five feet away from James Brown. Everybody should go to Vegas once in their lifetime. Some say three days is enough, but I say take a week, see all the shows, do it properly.

While I was back in England briefly Tanya's friend Julie went out to Hollywood to stay with her there. Tanz phoned to tell me that the

Previous pages
Left: With Brad Pitt and Guy Ritchie at the premiere of Snatch, Los Angeles, 2001.

Top right: With Quentin Tarantino at the Hollywood premiere of Snatch.

Bottom right: Tanya and me having a laugh with Guy Ritchie and Madonna at the Evening Standard Film Awards, 2000.

pair of them had been sunbathing topless by the pool, chatting away, when they heard someone call from the stairs to the house next door, beyond a tall hedge, 'Hi there! Are you the new neighbours?' Imagine the girls' faces as they looked up and realised that they were living next door to Pete Sampras and his new missus, Bridgette Wilson. Some neighbourhood! Rachel Hunter was the other side, Eddie Murphy was about ten houses away. At the top of the road were Warren Beatty and Jack Nicholson. Oh yes, and Cher had a house in the area, too.

Another mate, Clifford Edwards, came over in the summer holidays with his three boys, real jack-the-lads. I suppose they were about seven, eight and nine. I got a call from Brad Pitt inviting me round for a game of poker. I said to Clifford: 'Fancy a game of cards? We're going round to Brad Pitt's place.'

'Pack it in, you daft bugger,' he said.

His face when we got round there was a picture. There was Brad, cracking open a few beers for us and a couple of his actor pals as we waited for Guy Ritchie and Matthew Vaughn to arrive. Clifford was actually sitting next to Brad. He kept glancing over at me and tapping me with his foot under the table. There was a slight delay with the card school. It was gone midnight by the time Matthew turned up and announced: 'I've just had to drop Guy off. Madonna's been rushed in – she's ready to pop.'

When the phone rang later we could all hear Guy's delight as he shouted: 'It's arrived! A baby boy – Rocco.'

Brad Pitt opened some champagne and we all drank to the baby, to Madonna and to Guy. We were the first to know, and Clifford was right there in the middle of it all. It was hardly surprising that the next morning he told his boys: 'You know when you go back to school and have to write about what you did in the summer holidays? Well, if you say you got on a plane, flew to America, stayed in Hollywood for two weeks at Vinnie and Tanya Jones's house and your dad went to play cards at Brad Pitt's, they're likely to throw you out for lying. What you'll have to say is that we went to Southend in a caravan and played draughts and it rained every day. I can't believe what really happened, so the teachers certainly won't.'

The filming of *Swordfish* took about eight months. I had a new assistant on this movie. Having spent such a long time together it was understandable that Colesy and I needed a break from one another, and he settled back in England with a girlfriend. So I took Neil Digweed, who has now become my full-time assistant. Neil, who is in his forties, is a friend from some time back, and solid as a rock. Like Colesy, Neil was back and forwards to the airport on a regular basis, picking up members of the families and Tanz and the kids whenever they had the chance to be with me.

A big four-wheel-drive was provided this time. A tanker comes round and fills your vehicle at the studio every day if necessary.

Nice, eh?

I met John Travolta the day shooting started. We were preparing for a big scene in a nightclub with everybody present, including some 300 extras. John shook hands with every member of the cast and told them all: 'Hi, thanks for doing this film.' You could hear people almost gasping, 'Wow, what a pro.'

Travolta is a different type of bloke from Nick Cage. Just as pleasant, but you sense you could ask him anything. I said to him once: 'You're the captain of the ship as far as this operation is concerned, you can call the shots and do your own thing, and yet you spend so much time with so many people over there in your trailer.'

'I have to,' he told me. 'They all want a piece of you. Don't forget, I knew the bad times. I was down on the floor not so long ago, until *Pulp Fiction* brought me back. In this town, in this business, you have to keep your friends close and your enemies even closer.'

Travolta needs to get to know you before you feel a part of his circle. We ended up getting on brilliantly – as well as he does with his Australian co-star, Hugh Jackman.

The bigger the film, the more sitting around you do, and that's the hardest part. It drains you mentally. Most days you're on the set by eight in the morning. My role, as the lead mercenary of a group of five who attempt to nick a whole load of money from a CIA slush fund, made me Travolta's right-hand man. It was another action movie, so there was not too much dialogue to deal with, and I often had nothing to do until four in the afternoon. They operated what they call a twelve-hour turn-around – if you don't finish until seven at night, you can't be called back before seven the next morning. For night filming, I'd be picked up at four in the afternoon and dropped off home again at four in the morning.

So they were twelve-hour days, mostly, but when you weren't

involved in any of the scenes they were planning to film you could have, say, a week off on standby. This sometimes meant taking careful precautions. For instance, mobile phones didn't get a signal where we played golf at Malibu, so I had to leave the golf club number with the studio. Mind you, there's something quite appealing about a steward arriving by the side of your buggy with the message: 'Mr Jones, phone call. You need to be on the film set in an hour.'

My trailer was more of a mobile home: lounge, double bed, bathroom, shower, kitchen, TV, hi-fi. As soon as you arrive there, everyone is running after you. 'Coffee, Mr Jones? Breakfast?' All your costumes for the day are already laid out. In my case, five suits. The other mercenaries were sharing small trailers like the one I'd had on *Sixty Seconds*, so everybody and his aunt finished up in mine. It was like being back at the youth club. The boys would come round to watch films, enjoy drinks from the fridge, play backgammon or chess or just to have a bloody good chinwag and a joke. Not Travolta, though. He had more than enough to occupy him, with cooks, minders and a gym in his own private 'village'.

I think I became the most popular fella on the set with everybody: make-up girls, wardrobe, lighting and sound boys, actors and producers. I had a terrific thirty-sixth birthday. You couldn't get in my trailer for presents. Vases, DVDs, golf balls, tennis balls, champagne, T-shirts. Steve Jones gave me a big painting of the Sex Pistols, which I've had shipped back to England. Tanya bought me a fabulous bracelet.

Oops, almost forgot to mention

Claudia. Claudia Schiffer. She bought me a massage machine. A fairly large job, capable of treating the legs, back and so on. We got to know Claudia very well – she often came up to the house to play tennis – and we regard her among our friends.

My birthday bash was held at the trendy Sunset Room, a lovely restaurant and nightclub with a VIP area. Somehow, a story got around back home that Madonna was organising some strippers for it. Tanya was said to have been upset and to have threatened to call off the party. Not a word of it was true. Guy and Madonna weren't even coming to the party, for a start. Where do some people get their information? Anyway, I asked Neil who he thought we

should invite and he said: 'Invite everybody, and see what happens.' So I invited a whole load of people, including Jerry Bruckheimer, Nick Cage, Rod Stewart, John Travolta and Hugh Jackman. Dominic was good enough to film my scene early that day 'so you can get off to your party'. When Tanya and I arrived, Rod, Claudia, Steve Jones and Nick Cage were already there.

At midnight there was a bit of a commotion when the big man himself strolled in. It was John Travolta, with his missus. He brushed past everybody, asking: 'Where's the man? Where's Vinnie? Where's Tanya?' And we sat with them for ages. I thought it was a magnificent gesture, John Travolta accepting an invitation to my birthday party. I like to think it was a kind of seal of approval, especially in front of the other big names around us, and I whispered to Tanz: 'This shows we do have some credibility out here.'

Some birthday. Some night.

We didn't get to bed until eight in the morning.

I'd arranged for two lads from a little Irish bar to play the guitar and sing. And there I was, out in the middle of the dance floor with Tanya, with John Travolta and his wife, and Rod Stewart and Claudia Schiffer, dancing nearby. I sometimes pinch myself. It's a long way from washing pots and pans for a living to be able to pop round to Guy and Madonna's house at the bottom of the road, press the buzzer and hear her call: 'Hi Vinnie, come in. I'll put the kettle on.'

It was a pity we couldn't be at Guy and Madonna's wedding in Scotland, especially as he'd done me the honour of asking me to be his best man. But it was impossible because we were still deeply involved in the filming of *Swordfish*. I was, however, home for something that had been set up completely without my knowledge. I was in no way prepared for the moment Michael Aspel walked up to me and said: 'Vinnie Jones, This is Your Life.' I'd always dreamed that one day it might be me, but because of some of the controversies I'd been involved in, I never thought I'd get a sniff. So although I was puzzled as to why Neil had seemed so preoccupied and why Tanya was phoning Peter Burrell five times a day, the penny hadn't dropped.

When Michael Aspel walked in, I felt very strange. I kind of looked right through him and my eyes swam. I glanced down at the Red Book and it was the size of a Range Rover. Then the reality

Previous pages: My thirty-sixth birthday party in LA: with Hilton, Ian, Stewart and Mickey; Rod Stewart; John Travolta and his wife Kelly Preston; and enjoying a quieter moment with Tanya.

Caught out by
Michael Aspel and
his Red Book...

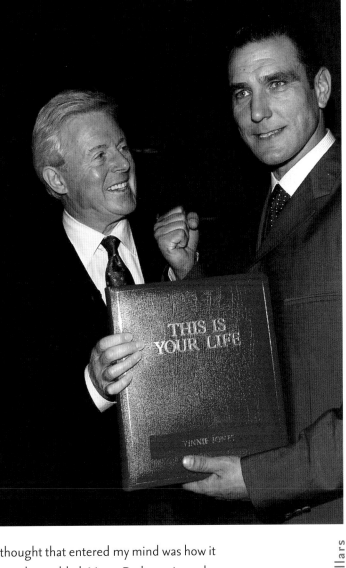

began to kick in. The first thought that entered my mind was how it would please Tanz, my nan and granddad, Mum, Dad, my sister, the kids and Tanya's family. It was a sensational night. So many old friends and acquaintances, even my old headmaster; so many memories and emotions, not least those stirred by Darren, a young lad who lost his sight in a road accident. We've kept in touch for years, ever since I bought him a trained guide dog.

This is Your Life makes you feel many things. Chuffed, proud, extremely happy and sometimes a little sad. But, with Tanya sitting beside me, my overall feeling was a sense of real satisfaction. I've always said I've worked bloody hard for what I've achieved, and when so many people take so much trouble to pay tribute to you, I

With Tanya, my dad
Peter and stepmum
Jenny at the GQ
Awards, 2000.

At the Brit Awards,
2000.

think you are entitled to believe that your efforts have been well and truly justified.

I wouldn't want to categorise myself as a star even though they call me a celebrity. For whatever reason, right, wrong, my fault or someone else's, I am a name. I am instantly recognisable and, would you believe, even when I was playing at Chelsea John Major and his son actually asked to meet me. I've been known to sit next to Tony Blair and natter away with him no differently from the way I'd chat to the lads at the local.

I have friends who are lords and friends on the dole, and I've managed to keep a balance between the two. I've grown up a great deal. I can no longer say: 'Well, I'm just a youngster and I'm mad,' although the Bedmond Green estate still comes out in me occasionally.

I have to admit that Vinnie Jones has been a thug at times, on and off the football field. I can't sit here and say I'm whiter than white. But whatever the task, needlework or fighting somebody, I'll always have a go. I can't be defeated before I've tried. I feel that I have been honest with myself, with my family, my managers and team-mates, with my animals and my friends. When I look back I don't feel I have deceived anybody.

I hope there's a lot more to come from my new career. I've already started having voice lessons in the States. I had a little bit of coaching for *Sixty Seconds* with Robert Eastern, a very famous guy out there, and more recently with Jess Platt, who coached Michael Caine, to prepare me for the next big challenge in the United States. It's a difficult process, because the American accent is so alien to me. There are hundreds of exercises involved in mastering even tiny adjustments. Jess gives me sheets and sheets of words, and then sentences. But you can't do more than an hour at a time. I practise as I go about my day-to-day business or when I'm just wandering about the house. I know how important the training could be in terms of opening new avenues.

Just as important as my past has been. In the scenes I have acted in on film, I've been able to draw from my own memory bank. I have been involved in, or seen, most things. I'm quite worldly and regard myself as very streetwise. If you can deliver a given set of circumstances for real, I think you have a chance as a professional actor.

As ever, I'm trying my best.